BEYOND THE BARRE

SARAH WILLIAMS

Serenade Publishing

To my partner Tim
For your support, patience and love.

SARAH WILLIAMS

LOVE STORIES THAT WILL ROPE YOU IN

CHAPTER 1

*S*carlett Matthews studied her figure in the long floor-to-ceiling mirrors in the dance studio. Six months after her final performance with the Queensland Ballet and her turnout was still as good as it ever had been, but she could see the extra padding on her hips and thighs that she hadn't had before. A lot had changed since moving to the country town of Maleny. Not just her figure, but her entire lifestyle. She was teaching ballet now instead of performing it herself on a stage in front of thousands.

She stood in the middle of the studio, wearing her usual uniform of a black leotard, tights, and ballet shoes. These items were like a second skin to her. She loosened her shoulders, rounded her arms into first position, and turned her feet out to match. With her classes finished for the day, and the studio quiet after the last of the teenagers had left, Scarlett danced a brief arabesque and spun on her demi-pointes. Her ballet shoes skimming over the dance floor to an imaginary tune.

Damn, she missed it—the glitter of stage lights reflecting off sequins, the thunder of the audience's applause, the thrill of mastering a new part. There was nothing else in her heart except ballet, nothing else she was passionate about. It was ballet or bust. Sometimes she feared that her soul might wither up and die if she went much longer without dancing. That was why she had taken up the role of ballet teacher at her friend Audrey's dance school. Now, instead of learning and dancing choreography, she was teaching it to young students who likely would never progress to a professional level.

After approaching the barre, she lifted her leg, resting her ankle on it and leaning out and over to stretch in a perfect line. Her muscles released as she stretched farther. She wasn't yet ready to give up the flexibility and grace that she had spent her lifetime working on. Years of stretching had given her a perfect curve en pointe.

"The others are waiting for us," Lilly called from the door of the studio.

Scarlett looked at the clock on the wall. The staff Christmas Party would already be in full swing up the road at the Bunya Bar, and she and Lilly had promised to join after finishing their classes and closing for the night.

"I'll just get changed. I'll be five minutes." Scarlett smiled at her friend before switching position to stretch her other leg.

After changing out of her leotard and tights and into black pants and her favourite pink T-shirt, Scarlett joined her colleague.

"You're not going to take down your hair?" Lilly asked.

Scarlett raised her hand and touched the neat bun. The hairspray and gel had kept it neatly in place during all the day's lessons. "I always wear my hair up. It feels weird to let it down."

She looked at Lilly's jet-black hair, cut in a cute modern bob. Lilly taught tap and although she was an amazing dancer in that style, she didn't have the discipline of a ballerina, where not a hair could be out of place, nor a stocking possess the slightest run.

"You should try it some time. It'd look cute." Lilly locked the studio door behind them as they headed out into the humid December night.

The walk to the Bunya Bar was a short one, and the women chatted about their day as they made their way through town. Around them, all the shops and cafes were closed, with only the occasional streetlamp illuminating the footpath.

The bar soon came into view. Light and noise flooded from the windows. Scarlett smoothed down the front of her shirt and pasted on her brightest smile. *Showtime!*

The historic building was decorated like most country pubs, with a timber floor and half-panelled timber walls. A series of tables were arranged to the left of the entrance, their wooden tops marked with drink rings and coasters. Several groups of men and women occupied the seats, and Scarlett glanced around but didn't see their party.

"They're in the beer garden," Lilly said and waved her on, past a door leading to the pokie-machine room. Past the bar to the right, on a plain carpeted area, stood a pool table lit by a long, low-hung light. Television screens showing racing odds sat high above a corkboard with racing fields tacked to it and a counter containing rows of betting slips. Several older men with long grey beards looked them up and down with appreciative stares as they passed, and Scarlett couldn't help the shiver that their ogling caused.

Of course, she was used to being watched and studied on stage. She was a performer and that was her job. But away from the bright lights and makeup, she preferred not to be the centre of attention. Being a ballerina came with too many expectations and fantasies, and she was always afraid to disappoint.

That was why she had always preferred the company of fellow dancers. They had more things in common with her than other people, and they knew the demands of her work. Spotting Audrey at a table outside with the rest of the staff and their partners, Scarlett and Lilly walked over and joined them. Scarlett greeted them all with handshakes and polite hugs before taking a seat with Lilly at the big picnic table.

Contemporary and jazz teacher Beth was there with her husband, Johno; Mariah was in her early twenties and taught hip-hop; and Audrey, also a ballet teacher, was sitting next to her fiancé, Wes.

"We should place our orders soon. There's already a big wait." Audrey handed Scarlett a menu, and Scarlett looked it over. "In the meantime, I ordered some garlic bread."

Carb-heavy meals of pasta and meat and rice dishes glared back at Scarlett. Skipping over the mains, she searched for a healthy option and was relieved when she found a simple house salad.

A waitress squeezed past Scarlett and placed a wicker basket on the table in front of her. "Here's some garlic bread while you're deciding."

The buttery smell teased Scarlett's nose. She knew it was silly, freaking out over one tiny slice of bread, but she couldn't help it. She'd spent years counting every precious morsel she allowed between her lips, calculating calories and fat units, knowing that the slightest slip-up would edge her further and further away from her goal weight. Not to mention the chance to be principal in the next performance.

A prickle of rebellion clawed through her. How long had it been since she'd tasted bread? Or chocolate or ice cream?

Damn. Ice cream.

Her mouth salivated at the thought. Real ice cream, not that fat-free, taste-free frozen yogurt she sometimes kept in the freezer at home for a treat.

Years. It had to have been years.

Beside her, Wes offered her the basket. "Grab a piece before they're gone."

Scarlett moved her hands below her bottom, sitting on them in order to stop herself from claiming a piece of the golden, yeasty goodness. "No, thanks." She shook her head.

The friends shared lively conversation, and Scarlett's body started to relax against the chair as she sipped her soda water and laughed at the stories being shared.

The tantalising aroma of barbecued steak teased her as it was placed in front of Wes. He eagerly reached for his knife and fork before cutting into it. Scarlett couldn't turn away from the meal as the juices flowed from the dissected meat.

Swallowing hard, she refocused her attention on the greens in front of her. Picking her way through the lettuce, she tried to imagine just what steak tasted like. It had been so long; she couldn't even remember.

"Linc! Over here." Wes paused his chewing to wave someone over.

The object of his attention turned, and Scarlett gazed appreciatively at the tall, ginger-haired man. He moved with long strides towards their table. His broad shoulders and narrow hips had all the girls looking up in silent approval, but it was his eyes that held Scarlett transfixed. Their light green was a shade she'd never seen before.

"Oh my gosh, he looks a bit like Prince Harry," Lilly whispered beside her. Scarlett did the mental comparison, and yes, her friend was right. He looked like the British royal, with his freckles and pink cheeks. She'd never seen such gingery-red hair up close. It suited him, of course, but she wondered if he had endured a childhood of teasing and bullying simply because he was born that way.

Wes stood and shook the man's hand before turning to the group for introductions. "This is Lincoln Buchanan, owner of Sunshine Brew. Maleny's best craft beer." He introduced everyone, finishing with Scarlett, who smiled shyly.

Did Lincoln's gaze linger just a little longer on her than was socially appropriate?

"I saw that article in the *Hinterland Times*," Mariah said. "You're getting ready to open your first bar soon."

Pride glimmered in Linc's eyes as he answered, "Yes, I'm hoping to open for New Year's Eve. So far, we're on schedule."

"I'll make sure to come by and check it out," Lilly said with a flirty smile. Did she actually flutter her eyelashes at him?

"Are you all dance teachers?" Linc asked with a grin that could melt the panties right off a woman.

Around her, the ladies nodded, most just as speechless as Scarlett.

"Scarlett here is our newest recruit." Audrey smiled at her. "She helps me with the ballet classes. In fact, your niece Aimee is in her class."

"Is that right?" Linc's gaze again lingered on her. "Is she as much of a handful in class as she is at home?"

Scarlett swallowed hard, forcing herself to think about the sweet little eight-year-old girl from her grade one class. "Aimee is a lovely girl. She pays attention and picks up the steps very quickly."

She was aware of Audrey's gaze skimming between the two of them, and the cocked eyebrows of their friends as they watched the interaction unfold.

"You'll be able to see for yourself at the Christmas concert," Audrey said. "You are coming, aren't you?"

Linc's gaze finally left Scarlett's, and he turned to Audrey. "Christmas concert? Oh yeah, right, of course I'll be there."

"Excellent," Audrey said as she turned back to Scarlett, and Linc was pulled into conversation with Wes. "Be careful with that one," she whispered for her ears only.

"What do you mean?" Scarlett tried hard not to gaze too longingly at the man. He really was very sexy in those jeans.

"I adore Linc, but he could charm the skin off a snake. And he knows how good-looking he is. He's every woman's type."

Lilly leaned in beside them and said in a hushed voice, "He's definitely mine."

Scarlett shook her head and tossed the comment away. "I'm not looking to get involved with anyone. My life is busy enough as it is."

The girls exchanged a look and a murmur. Scarlett picked up her drink and sipped it, her eyes taking another peek of Linc over the rim of her glass.

"It was lovely meeting you all," Linc said, raising his hand in a brief wave. "Enjoy the rest of your night."

They farewelled him in return before he walked back to the bar, re-joining a group of men.

If she hadn't still been staring after him, Scarlett would have missed the way he positioned himself so she was still in his eyeline. Occasionally, throughout the evening, she would look up and their gazes would meet, or he would send her a smile that could only be called seductive.

But a man like Linc was not on the agenda. She had sworn off men for good. It would be a spinster's life for her. She would not let herself be hurt a second time. She was still recovering from her last heartbreak and could not risk another.

As nice as it was to be receiving some male attention, one thing was very clear in her mind: she would not be talking to Linc again. That was one decision she was firm on.

An absolute no-brainer.

Lincoln Buchanan wasn't the sort of guy to daydream about a woman he barely knew. He was decisive and strong-willed. When he saw something he wanted, he went for it and, more often than not, he would succeed.

He knew it wasn't luck that made him that way. It was sheer determination and confidence that made for a thriving new business with orders he was hard-pressed to keep up with. It was also his charm and experience that kept a new, warm female in his bed most nights.

So, what was it about the new dance teacher? Why couldn't he get her out of his mind?

She wasn't even his type. Curvy, carefree tourists looking for a fun night out were more his style. Certainly not a local, as new to town as she might be. *Don't shit where you eat* was a rule he had tried to hold fast to. As a business owner, he didn't need the town gossips causing any trouble or speculating over a future Mrs Buchanan.

Like he would ever get married. What a joke!

Besides, Scarlett was too small and dainty for him. She was like a porcelain doll he would too easily crush in his large hands. And didn't ballerinas have a reputation for being snobs? She certainly had appeared to look down her nose at him with those silvery-grey eyes of hers.

Eyes he would like to lose himself in. Cheeks he

would like to stroke, and those full red lips. Oh, he wanted to know how they tasted so badly!

And that was how he came to find himself strolling up to the Hinterland Dance Academy the following Tuesday afternoon.

During their weekly family lunch on Sunday, Linc had mentioned meeting Aimee's ballet teacher. The little girl had been so excited she had launched into great depth about when her lessons were and how often she practised, and had even demonstrated some moves she had been learning.

Linc had listened intently, storing away all the offered information about Scarlett, then casually tossed out the offer to pick her up one day if her parents were pressed for time. The space he was renting for his new bar was, conveniently, just a few doors away and it wouldn't be a problem at all. His brother Brad had exchanged a brief look with his wife, Mandy, before jumping at the opportunity.

Linc checked his watch. He was a good ten minutes early and the studio waiting room was empty as he entered. Soft piano music played, and he followed the noise, hoping to hear that pretty voice again.

Luck appeared to be on his side as he spotted an internal window and peeked through to see a class in session. Eight girls in pink leotards, tights, and ballet shoes skipped around in a circle before splitting into two groups and twirling on their toes.

"That's it, girls." Scarlett's voice rang from the front of the room and he moved to better see her.

Dressed in a black leotard, tights, and pink ballet shoes, she looked every bit the professional ballerina. The simplicity of her pulled back hair showcased the high curve of her cheekbones.

Then she was moving across the floor, rising on her toes, and leaping gracefully.

"She's amazing to watch, isn't she?"

What the—oh. Audrey stood behind him, studying him. When had she arrived?

He cleared his throat before answering. "I don't know much about ballet, but she seems to know what she's doing."

"Scarlett was one of the best at the Queensland Ballet. We're very lucky to have her. She could have danced professionally for a few more years instead of accepting this job."

He glanced back through the window as the class wrapped up and the students curtsied to her. "Can they see us?" He waved at the window.

"No, it's one-way glass. So parents can watch without being a distraction." Audrey turned to open the classroom door and the little ballerinas streamed out, noisily chatting about their class and all they had learned.

Aimee spotted him and flung her arms around his waist. "Uncle Linc, did you watch me?"

He patted her gently on the back. "I saw a little bit. You did great."

"Who's bottle is this?" Scarlett appeared in the doorframe, holding up a pink water bottle. Her eyes found him and she stilled. "Oh, it's you."

"It's mine," Aimee said, releasing him and skipping to Scarlett, who handed it over. "Look, my Uncle Linc is here."

"I see that." Scarlett smiled at the girl before turning back to him. "Hi again."

He smiled, hoping he looked sexy but scared it appeared goofy. Shit, he was really off his game with this woman. "That seemed to be a good lesson."

Scarlett looked at the window in front of him, her eyes widening. "You watched?"

"I got here early. I hope you don't mind."

Her cheeks were a healthy pink, her lips pink and plump. Even though the mascara was gone, her lashes were naturally long and dark enough to feather over the top of her cheeks. A pair of simple silver earrings studded her ears, but she wore no other jewellery that he could see. She paused briefly before answering. "No, I mean, that's what it's there for. I just forget sometimes. I'm so focused on the class."

"You look really good." The words tumbled out of his mouth. "I mean, the girls looked really good. I was impressed."

"Thanks." She turned back toward the door. Now

that she was side on, he couldn't help but look at her again. Her tights left nothing to the imagination. She had a curved bottom and long, muscular legs. The faintest indents of her ribs showed below two tiny bumps on her chest. An athlete's body for sure. Not a gram of excess body fat that he could see. He'd bet she looked sexy as hell in one of those pancake ballerina tutus.

"I'd better get ready for the next class. Aimee, good job today. I'm so proud of how far you've come."

Aimee looked up from the floor where she was pulling off her leather shoes. A grin split her face. "Thank you, Ms Scarlett."

Linc smiled at the teacher as she glanced briefly at him before walking back into the studio.

"How many days a week do you take these lessons?" he asked his niece.

"Tuesdays and Thursdays."

He nodded as he watched through the window. Scarlett went to her bag and pulled out a water bottle. Her neck extended as she wrapped those luscious lips around it and drank deeply.

He'd never been with a ballet teacher before, and he couldn't help but wonder if she could teach him a thing or two. He wouldn't mind being under her private tutelage, and the more he thought about it, the more he wanted her.

She was a prize that wouldn't easily be won, but he was sure the challenge would be worth the result.

CHAPTER 2

*L*inc rubbed his eyes before staring back at the computer screen in front of him. Around him, the machinery thrummed its way through a cycle. Everything in the brewing process had to be exact or else the finished product wouldn't taste right, and he would be out the entire cost of the brew. It was tedious, calculated work. But he loved it. And the end result was a variety of craft beers that customers loved and kept ordering.

Linc could have sold the business several times by now. Instead, he'd chosen to take it to the next level by opening his own bar. After all, he had spent a lot of his adult years in pubs, bars, and nightclubs, and he knew what customers wanted. Good quality beer, tasty food, and a lively atmosphere. That was exactly what he planned to give them when Sunshine Brew opened on New Year's Eve.

As the machines finished their cycle and came to a quiet stop, Linc could hear the builders in the next room, hammering away. Soon the space would be fitted out with a sleek, modern bar, display cases, tables, and chairs. He had also planned a stage and had already booked a local band for their opening night. Everyone he spoke to was excited about the new venue. As good as the Bunya Bar was, it was struggling to cope with the growing crowds and tourists attracted to Maleny for the scenic countryside, cool climate, and quaint country shops and attractions.

"Here you are."

Linc turned at the sound of Wes's voice and greeted him with a smile. "Hey, mate, what's going on?"

Wes gestured at the large metal vats lined up along the walls. "You've come a long way from those bottles of home brew you used to make us drink."

Linc chuckled at the memory. He had thought he'd known everything back in his youth. Oh, how much he'd learned. "Yep, it's all paying off now. Want to try my latest recipe?"

When Wes eagerly nodded, Linc led him to the tasting area he had set up next to a fridge. Wes sat on the stool and leaned against the empty barrel, which served as a table. Linc pulled out two beer glasses before retrieving an unmarked bottle from the fridge. "You're one of the first to try this. I pureed local straw-berries and rhubarb and added them into the fermenter in the secondary fermentation, after the malt sugars had been consumed." He poured the light pink liquid into the two glasses.

"Sounds like a chick drink," Wes said sceptically.

"Just try it. I'd like your opinion."

Both men sipped their drinks.

"You can taste the strawberry, but it's dry and sharp. Almost like a dry rose wine." Wes nodded. "Audrey and her staff will love it. Especially if you can make it low calorie."

Linc nodded, the idea taking seed. Low-calorie alcohol was definitely a trend, especially with the hipsters, and they made up a big part of his target market. "Great idea. Thanks."

They finished their drinks while chatting about the bar and his plans for it.

"I can't wait. I'll be here New Year's Eve and I reckon most of town will be too." Wes checked his watch. "I better go. Audrey has me building a dance floor for the Christmas festival. The dancers need a particular floor or apparently they could injure themselves. Plus, Audrey thought it'd be fun if the teachers did a little performance of their own. Show the students how the professionals do it. Maybe give them something to work towards."

Linc nodded, trying not to let the rising excitement show on his face. "So, um, all the teachers will dance?"

Wes nodded. "Yep."

"Do you need any help?" The words tumbled out of his mouth.

"Aren't you busy enough?"

Linc shook his head. Actually, he was extremely busy with only three weeks until opening, and Christmas and Boxing Day holidays taking up precious time. But the thought of being able to see Scarlett again made it all worth it. If he helped out, he was bound to bump into her.

"Never too busy to give my friends a hand."

"Thanks. We could use all the help we can get."

Linc had been working on the stage for a solid hour, with no sign of a certain ballerina. Sweat dripped from his face as he nailed pieces of timber together to form the frame of the mobile stage. Usually the end-of-year concert was performed inside the community centre, in the air-con, but this year the centre was closed for refurbishment and the dance school had been asked to perform as part of the annual Christmas festival. The entire Main Street would be closed to traffic, and stalls would be erected selling food and locally made products. Sideshow alley would help to keep children entertained with various stands such as laughing clowns and lucky ducks to tempt willing participants.

"Excuse me, Lincoln?" The sweet strains of a woman's voice pulled him from his thoughts, and he looked over his shoulder to see Scarlett dressed in black bike shorts and a purple singlet. Bare ivory skin shimmered under the bright shine of the sun.

Linc swallowed hard and pulled his gaze from her long bare legs up to her face, which was partially hidden by the visor of her sun cap.

He thought back to the videos he had found online of her dancing. He'd trawled through photos of her performing en pointe and even found a video of one of her Australian Ballet performances and watched it, enraptured. *It's not stalking if you're looking up someone famous,* he'd convinced himself.

Dropping the hammer and nails, he straightened up. "Hi, Scarlett."

"Hello," she said, tucking a wisp of hair behind her ear and surveying the frame before her. "This is coming together well. Did you do it all yourself?"

Unintentionally, Linc's chest puffed out just a bit. "Yeah. Still a way to go yet though."

"I wondered if you could help me for a bit? Audrey bought an enormous tree—a real one—and I need to decorate it." She looked away shyly. "It's just I'm a little scared of heights."

A smile split his face. What other interesting facts might he learn about this mysterious woman? "No problem. Let's go."

He followed her through a gate at the back of the dance studio to a courtyard. There stood a huge green pine tree secured in a pot filled with soil. He looked at the top of the tree, which had to be close to three metres high. No wonder Scarlett didn't want to climb up there. If he wasn't trying to impress her, he wasn't sure he would either.

"The ladder is here." She gestured to the fence where the ladder stood next to several plastic boxes labelled *decorations.*

Nodding, Linc prepared the ladder, and they discussed how to drape the lights and tinsel around the giant.

For the next hour, he went up and down the ladder. When Scarlett's fingers brushed his as she passed him a small silver star, her cheeks coloured before she bent to collect another ornament. He concentrated on hanging the star and not on the sudden need to link his fingers with hers to prolong the contact.

Standing so close to her, feeling the care in her touch, only stripped away another layer of his self-control. The need to take her in his arms and kiss her was so intense, it took all of his willpower to appear casual and unmoved. He'd never been more relieved than he was when her hand had lowered and she'd moved away.

"What are your plans for Christmas?" he asked as he paused at the bottom of the tree.

"I guess I'll visit my mum in Brisbane." She shrugged. "I'm not really that into Christmas. I was always so busy dancing in the annual performance of *The Nutcracker* that by the time Christmas Day came, I slept most of it."

"What was it like?"

"Dancing?"

He nodded, intrigued by her past and all the reasons she had turned into this woman. She appeared small and fine-boned. Then her head lifted, and she looked straight at him. Any impression of fragility evaporated.

"Long hours; hard work. We trained like athletes and got plenty of injuries to prove it."

His heart clenched as he thought of her injured and in pain.

Then she smiled in that wistful, dreamy way, like she was remembering a particularly pleasant dream. "From the moment I put on my first ballet shoes, it was the only thing I ever wanted to do."

When Scarlett smiled like that, her eyes shone a brilliant grey. It wasn't just their clarity that stalled his thoughts but the expression within them. Sweet. Serene. Real. He could free fall in such eyes.

Once the tree was adorned in all its silver and red glory, they stepped back to admire their work. But as eye-catching as the tree was, Linc was only aware of the woman who stood beside him. Of her subtle floral scent. Of the full curve of her bottom lip.

"It's beautiful," she said as she gazed upon it.

"Yes, it is." His eyes were unable to leave Scarlett's face.

"What's next then?"

"I'd like to take you out to dinner." The words fell out of his mouth.

Her eyes widened. "Um, that's really sweet of you to ask, Linc, but—"

Shit. Nothing good ever followed a but. What was wrong with him today? He never got a but. Women were always putty in his hands. He was the one turning them down.

"Are you seeing someone?" It was the only possible explanation.

"No." She shook her head and crossed her arms over her chest. "I'm just not dating anymore."

"What? Why?"

Her gaze lowered to study the ground. "I'm sorry. I'm just not up to it. Plus, I'm so busy with the dance recital and work." She shrugged. "I should go."

She had a carefully constructed veneer that held him at arm's length. A woman with a mystery was his personal weakness, and there was a hell of a lot more to her story than she was letting on. He was drawn in by the opportunity to discover her secrets, to peel away the layers of complexity that shrouded her.

"Scarlett?" He reached out to touch her. His hand barely skimmed the warm, smooth curve of her shoulder. "I'm sorry for whatever it was that made you feel that way. I can wait until you're ready."

"Thanks, but please don't. You'd be wasting your time." She hurried away from him then and he was left standing in front of the Christmas tree with even more questions about the beautiful ballerina.

CHAPTER 3

The Hinterland Dance Academy's big day had arrived. The annual end-of-year recital was a showcase of all the routines they had been perfecting for months. It would be Scarlett's first time back on a stage since she'd left the Queensland Ballet. Memories flooded her, and the old thrill of adrenaline that came before a performance lit up her senses.

She peeked out from behind the red velvet curtain that Linc and Wes had erected as a backdrop for the stage. People were gathering on the grassy patch in front where folding chairs, hay bales, and picnic blankets had been placed for people to sit on or against and watch the performance.

Beyond the stage were rows of tables for people to sit and eat at. Potted poinsettias and tinsel adorned them. Fairy lights twinkled from where they decorated trees and the distant strains of a Christmas carol filled the air. Even the hardware store was smothered in tinsel with an inflatable Santa secured beside the front door.

She was nervous. No point denying it, even if only to herself. This was the first time she'd been responsible for the choreography and music choice. What if her students forgot their steps? What if the audience didn't enjoy it? It could all reflect badly on her and maybe she could even lose her job. Then there was the matter of the teacher dance and her small solo. She knew her ankles weren't as strong as they used to be—what if she fell on her fat ass and everyone saw? How embarrassed she would be.

Doing her best to push down her growing anxiety, she turned from the audience to cast her gaze over her students. Separated into groups, they were all dressed in colourful costumes with stage makeup on and hair tied tightly back, giggling to each other without a care in the world.

The first strains of the opening scene set the dancers into motion, their graceful forms taking the music and interpreting it into lyrical movement. The teenage girls moved to their well-rehearsed routine, drawing even more people to the audience.

Scarlett kept busy backstage with last-minute wisps of hair and smudged lipstick. She watched each of her groups perform without too many mistakes to a cheering audience of family and friends. The excitement of the concert drummed familiar adrenaline through Scarlett as she changed into her costume and slipped on her old pair of pointe shoes.

"Miss Scarlett?" Aimee's quiet voice came from behind her. "Will I get pointe shoes one day?" The child's gaze was fixed on one of Scarlett's well-worn shoes with its ribbons and squared off toes.

With a smile and a nod, Scarlett replied, "If you keep up with your lessons and practise, you sure will."

Aimee wrapped her arms around her teacher. The hug surprised Scarlett, who always maintained professionalism with all her students. But this hug, from this child, did something to ease her nerves.

"I want to be just like you when I grow up."

The sweetness of the child's words touched Scarlett's heart. From a distance, her life must have seemed so glamorous. Like she was living the dream.

When she danced, Scarlett left her real life behind. The ache in her knee and the callouses on her toes faded away as she allowed herself to go to that magical place where only the music and the movements mattered. When she was dancing, she wasn't anxious over her weight or her loneliness. It was the only way she knew how to escape her real life. A life that, when you looked closely enough, really wasn't all that glamorous after all.

The last group of students exited the stage to a clapping audience.

Scarlett stood, touched her hair, ensuring it was still

tightly pulled back, then made her way to the side where she would start her dance.

One at a time, the teachers took to the stage, dancing in their preferred style. To jazz music, Beth danced a funky routine, then Lilly tap-danced, her shoes click-clicking loudly on the stage. The music changed again and Mariah performed her hip-hop routine before Audrey started the ballet section. The music changed to a familiar classic, and Scarlett let herself be transformed into the dancer once again as she took to the stage.

Despite how cute the little kids were when they fluttered across the stage, the red velvet backdrop shimmering behind them, Linc wriggled in his seat. The sun was going down, bringing with it a welcome respite from the heat of the day. But the humidity clung to the air. Rain clouds had formed overhead, and he could only hope and pray that they didn't dispense their contents until after the show.

The festival was proving as popular as ever. People relaxed in chairs in front of the makeshift stage, enjoying the live music. Lines had formed outside the food venues, and the stalls were barely visible amongst the crowds milling around them.

"You don't have to stay," Linc's sister-in-law whispered beside him. "I'll video Aimee so you can watch it later."

Amongst the small crowd, he saw the proud faces of parents and grandparents and the excitement of younger siblings who had trouble staying in their seats. Tonight wasn't just about Christmas and family, but also about a small community celebrating its future.

He smiled back at her. "It's fine. I want to be here." And he did want to see his niece in her costume. But he wasn't just there for her.

Aimee's ballet routine was cute. The little girls pretended to be fairies with magical wings that let them fly. At least that was what Mandy said they were doing when they pretended to flap their arms.

His niece almost had the same whimsical expression on her face he had seen on Scarlett that day at the dance class. He hadn't been able to get his mind off Scarlett since they'd decorated the Christmas tree together. He had never felt like this. He liked commitment-free fun. Feelings were off-limits. He was still young and enjoyed his social life. He enjoyed meeting new women and their company, in and out of the bedroom and he always made them aware that their relationship wouldn't progress past a short fling.

Scarlett had said she didn't want to go out with him. He knew he should respect her wishes and stay away. If only he believed her. But when she looked at him, he knew she must feel it too. He was drawn to her like a moth to a flame. He needed to be in her atmosphere, if not her life. Behind those beautiful eyes were pain and loneliness, and he wanted to be the one to soothe them away.

"Now it's the teachers," someone beside him said, and he fixed his attention on the stage.

His experience with dance was fairly limited, but he appreciated the skill and technique these dancers possessed. They all took turns showing off their moves to a cheering audience.

Then the music changed to more classical piano, and the audience shushed as Scarlett took the stage. Dressed in a costume of deep royal blue, the bodice fitting her body like a second skin, with a matching blue tutu trimmed in white around the edges, Scarlett floated to the centre of the stage, her toes skimming the surface of the floor.

Her arms were rounded above her head, and she was all long lines and graceful curves. She moved with a dreamlike quality, ebbing like the ins and outs of the tide as she told a story with her body. Her face glowed and even from his seat in the second row, he could see her eyes sparkling.

She pirouetted several times, then took her final pose, and the crowd erupted into applause. Linc was the first to his feet, clapping and cheering. Others joined him until nothing else could be heard. Scarlett curtsied twice to the audience, her stage smile firmly in place. Then she was tiptoeing off the stage and back behind the curtain.

"Maybe you'll come to Aimee's recitals more often?" Mandy nudged him gently in the ribs.

Damn, he'd been so caught up and transfixed he'd forgotten to stay cool and collected. If his brother and sister-in-law suspected he had a crush, he would never live it down.

"Come on, even I could see the beauty and skill in that."

"Yes, and one particular ballerina caught your eye." Mandy smiled. "I never thought I'd see the day you finally fell for someone."

"I think you're seeing things. I barely know Scarlett."

"Not as well as you'd like to, at least." She spoke the words he had just been thinking. It was true. He would like to know her much better indeed.

Hoping to see Scarlett, Linc wandered up and down the street. He was pretending to be interested in the stalls but constantly looking back at the stage. He walked past a trio of reindeers shaped out of lights that stood in front of a large sleigh on which red and gold tinsel rippled in the breeze. Near them, three metal-crafted cows were artistically decorated with tinsel and baubles, festively welcoming people into the town so widely known for its dairy farms and locally produced milk products.

Emerald Hill was the biggest of the dairy farms, and the two sisters who ran it had done amazing things with the business, including farm tours and a much-loved gourmet restaurant. The farm had recently become the go-to wedding venue on the Sunshine Coast.

Linc was proud to be part of this community. Most people were supportive of new ventures and ideas, although a few of the older families missed the quieter years before the tourists, when their views were not obscured by housing estates. Maleny was a place outsiders wanted to move to and locals wanted to stay.

He stood in front of the bookstore and gazed around the street. Being summer, everyone was dressed in shorts and T-shirts. The sun set late these days, and the air held its warmth.

While in the northern hemisphere people would be enjoying hot cocoa or eggnog, here in Maleny the kids were sucking on flavoured icy-poles.

He chatted with some old friends as they passed and eventually decided to hunt Scarlett down. At least he had an excuse to see her. He wanted to congratulate her on the show and thank her for all her hard work teaching Aimee and her friends.

Wes and Audrey were stacking the last of the chairs when he returned, and he helped to load them onto the back of their ute. They chatted about the recital as they worked. It had been the last event for the year, and now the children had six weeks holiday. No more school or extracurricular activities.

"Remember when we spent all summer at Gardners Falls?" Linc asked Wes.

"How old were we when we started going there? Twelve?"

"We started going to watch the girls in their bikinis."

Wes caught Audrey looking at him with a cocked eyebrow. "And it was the only place we could swim to cool off," he said.

"Come on, you perv. Let's get this stuff back to the studio." Audrey waved her fiancé over, and they drove the ute down the street, away from the crowds.

Linc wandered around the stage. The curtain was still erected, as was a marquee behind which, judging from the hanging racks filled with costumes beside it, must have been used as a dressing room.

He spotted Scarlett, still in her leotard, but the tutu had been removed. Disappointment rushed through him. She had looked so damn good in it. Even now, with bike pants and running shoes on, she looked hot. He paused to take her in, but she must have sensed him as she looked up.

"Hi. Come to help pack up?" She smiled at him, exhaustion showing on her face. It must have been a busy, long day for all the staff involved, as well as the children.

"I'm at your disposal. How can I help?"

Scarlett gave him plenty to do from dismantling the marquee to putting costumes in plastic hanging bags. They chatted easily as they worked, and he was again surprised by just how comfortable he was in her company.

"How are the plans for the bar coming along?" she asked.

Linc zipped up another costume bag. "Everything is running pretty smoothly. I've had it planned out for a while though, so there haven't been any major surprises."

"That's good to hear. Do you still plan to open for New Year's Eve?"

"I do. Not much else happens that night around here, so everyone is pretty excited about it." Linc knew there was a lot riding on this. The bar would open with a bang, and he hoped nobody would be disappointed. He knew the beers would taste great. It was the other things, like the music and the food, that he couldn't control, and that worried him. He liked being in control. Though Scarlett didn't help him feel that way. As far as their relationship—or lack of it—went, she was definitely in charge.

He studied her face. It was artistically covered in stage makeup, which, although beautiful on her, didn't compare to her natural, clear skin. She was a beauty, and he wondered if she realised just how gorgeous she was. Surely she had been told a thousand times by fans and boyfriends. Although she didn't seem to be as egotistical as he would have expected a ballerina to be.

Like he himself sometimes was.

"Scarlett?" He stopped working and waited for her

to look at him. When she did, their eyes met and held. "Would you come to the opening with me?"

"On New Year's Eve?"

"Yes. As my... guest?" He had to move slowly with her. Move too fast and he was sure she would run and hide, never to be found again.

"Guest? So not a date?"

"Not if you don't want it to be. And lots of people will be there. It will be a great night."

He wished he could read her mind. He could almost see the cogs turning as she thought about his request.

She was getting to him, making him want to see what secret she kept so close to her chest, what pain she hid from the world. He was drawn to her in some primal, uncontrollable way. But there was nothing he could do to satiate that desire. Scarlett was complex. She played her cards close to her chest, and she hadn't asked him for a single thing. That put her in a special category all of her own, and that meant he couldn't treat her the way he treated others.

"You are persistent, aren't you?" she asked.

He shot her his most charming smile. "It's one of my many charming qualities."

Finally, she nodded. "Okay."

It was a simple answer, but he'd take it. "Great. Do you want me to pick you up?"

She shook her head. "No, you'll be busy setting up. I'll meet you there."

"Okay." He grinned and tried to suppress his excitement.

He couldn't wait to show her his bar and have her sample his beers. If she'd only let him, maybe then she'd finally agree to take a chance on the man who didn't normally want one.

CHAPTER 4

*C*hristmas was a quiet affair for Scarlett. Although she had been invited to spend the day with all the dance teachers and their families, she had decided to spend it alone, just as she had spent so many in her childhood.

It wasn't that her mother was negligent. She was encouraging and supportive of her only daughter, but once Scarlett had proven her maturity and that she could be left alone, her mother had created herself a new life. She had a full-time job, new friends—even a new husband.

Scarlett knew the cost of her dance lessons had been a major reason for this. Her mother had paid for three-hour lessons every day after school and eisteddfods on many weekends, not to mention the uniforms and cost of shoes. Scarlett pondered this as she made herself a chicken salad for lunch. Perhaps part of her drive to succeed had been so that her mother would pay her more attention. Would come to more of her events. Would tell her how proud she was.

She stabbed her fork into the dry salad. She'd been ten when her dance teacher had first sat her students down to have the food talk. She'd set a small silver scale on the table and showed them how to weigh out portions of food, right down to the handful of almonds they'd been instructed to eat as an afternoon snack.

A dancer had to be slender, she'd said. A dancer had to leap and soar as if they weighed nothing at all, and they couldn't very well do that with an extra ring of padding around their waist.

Scarlett remembered looking in the mirror that night, anxiously pinching at the baby fat still on her small body, imagining her partner straining to lift her up onstage. A dancer's instrument was her body, and Scarlett's had to be perfect.

Her baby fat had melted away, and with training and a careful diet, she'd hit her teens with a perfect dancer's build: lean, muscular, and lithe. She remembered overhearing her mother talking smugly with some other dance mums after rehearsals. "Of course, we don't have to worry about Scarlett's figure," her mother had said proudly. "She has discipline; she doesn't let herself go."

Then puberty had hit and suddenly, all the willpower in the world hadn't been able to stop the weight creeping in. New curves had developed where once she'd been so slim. The scales had gone back on the kitchen counter. Her teacher had designed a brutal new diet plan and cut out everything except the most necessary fuel.

Scarlett put the half-eaten salad in the fridge, pulled on her running shoes, and went for a jog. Old habits were hard to break, so she kept up the diet she had started in her teens and the daily exercise regime.

Out the door of her duplex, she turned left onto the deserted road and jogged her usual gruelling track up and down the steep hills of Maleny. As she passed the most scenic lakes and creeks, and lush green hills with dairy cows grazing, she let her thoughts drift to Lincoln.

How was he spending the day? He'd told her he would be with his family. Aimee was a lucky child to have such kind parents, and be surrounded by family and friends. Not the lonely childhood she'd had.

As if thinking about her mother had conjured her, Scarlett stopped running and pulled her ringing phone from her pocket.

"Merry Christmas, darling."

"Merry Christmas, Mum. How's your day going?"

"Good. We're in Sydney. Staying in Circular Quay."

"Oh, nice." Scarlett remembered the last time she had been to the largest Australian city. Her company had been touring the country, dancing *Giselle* to packed out theatres.

Scarlett walked while she and her mother chatted,

catching each other up on the last few weeks of their lives.

"Have you been going out much? Dating?"

"I had a work Christmas party a couple of weeks ago."

"You should put yourself out there more. Meet some people." Her mother sighed, "I'm not trying to push you. I'm just saying that it's okay to let your hair down every once in a while. You know—live a little. Maybe act like you're twenty-seven instead of seventy-seven."

Her words stung, but only because they were true. Scarlett was living the life of a hermit, but only because it was safe. She was still healing and recuperating from the last few years. This was the first time in her life when she didn't have high demands or expectations placed on her. She was finally resting, taking some time out just for her.

"I have been invited to the opening of a new bar on New Year's Eve."

"Really? Tell me more." Her mother's voice was filled with enthusiasm.

"The owner, Linc, invited me. It'll be a huge event."

"That sounds like so much fun. I'm really glad you're going. Are you and Linc dating?"

She couldn't help but let out a nervous laugh. "No, I barely know him. He makes craft beer for a living."

"He's an entrepreneur. Nothing wrong with that. Is he handsome?"

She didn't want to get her mother's hopes up that her only daughter was ready to settle down and have a family. Scarlett didn't see that scenario playing out anytime soon.

"Linc looks very similar to Prince Harry. The red hair and freckles." But those green eyes were like nothing she had ever seen before. Uniquely Lincoln.

"Very nice. Have you been going out long?"

""Mum," Scarlett groaned. "I told you, we're not dating. This is just a social event that the whole town is invited to."

"Well, I'm just glad you're going out. A small town like that probably doesn't offer much for you young ones. You should take all the opportunities you can get."

Scarlett found herself at the centre of town. No cars were moving through the main roundabout, so she could clearly see the large tree on the island in the centre. It was adorned with Christmas present ornaments, tinsel, and other colourful decorations.

After today, many locals would head to the various beaches or camping spots for a holiday week with their families. But Scarlett had no such plans. In fact, she had no plans at all. For the first time in her life, no one had demands or expectations of her. The Summer School program was a week away, and she had already prepared for the upcoming classes.

Maybe she should take up a new hobby? Or start reading more?

"Sweetheart, I've got to go, but have a wonderful time on New Year's Eve. I want to hear all about it."

"Ok, merry Christmas, Mum. I love you."

"Love you too, Scarlett. Bye." The phone call ended.

Scarlett put her phone back in her pocket and gazed around the empty streets. The day had heated up; the sun was high in the sky. She had better get indoors soon before she got sunburnt.

Maybe she would watch Christmas movies and daydream about her very own Prince Charming.

Christmas flew by in a blur of activity for Linc as his days got longer and anxiety set in. The closer the opening got, the more worried he was something would go wrong. What if the stock ran out? What if no one showed? Had he ordered enough chairs? Were his staff fully trained?

But now the night was in full swing he started to relax. Everything was progressing smoothly. The stars were out; the air was sweet and balmy; the band was great, and a few people had even started dancing.

He came out from behind the bar when he saw Wes heading his way. "Congratulations, man. This place is looking great." Wes clapped Linc on the back with his spare hand. The other gripped a pint of amber beer.

"Thanks." Linc looked out at the sizeable crowd, trying to get his head around how many people had shown up to support him and his venture. Their happy faces warmed his heart. This was exactly what he had wanted—to bring people together, to build community spirit. The last few years had been difficult for the town. Bushfires, floods, and other natural disasters were normal occurrences in country towns. Add in a pandemic and many shops and cafes had closed their doors, never to be reopened.

Two girls, dressed in denim shorts and barely anything else, strolled past them, giggling and smiling at Linc. From boyhood, Linc had possessed the sort of looks that made people stop and stare. By the time he'd reached adolescence, wherever he went, girls had swivelled so fast for a second glimpse that they tripped over their feet.

Linc had always loved the attention. Most people commented about his similar looks to the British Prince Harry, and he wasn't about to turn down such a compliment. The royal had made gingers popular. When once he might have been teased, now the girls loved his red hair, and it gave him a sense he was special. One of a kind.

Wes nudged him in the ribs. "You could take your pick tonight."

Linc took another look at the girls. He could probably have them both at once if he was so inclined. Keeping things casual had always been his jam. He had seen the way his parents were—so reliant on each other and needy. They could never do what they

wanted without getting the other's permission. He
didn't like that kind of control. He was in charge of his
life, and he'd never wanted to be responsible for
anyone else's happiness.

But tonight he wasn't thinking about getting laid.
Tonight was a special night, and he didn't want to start
the new year with a woman he probably wouldn't see
again. There were some boundaries you just didn't
cross, and this was one of them. New Year's was for
friends and family. Not one-night stands or flings.

Besides, he was waiting for a particular girl tonight.

He hadn't seen Scarlett come in yet.

They hadn't even exchanged phone numbers, so
he'd had no contact with her in more than a week.
Although he could have asked Audrey for her number,
he wanted to wait and let Scarlett decide she wanted to
give it to him. The last thing he should do was try to
put any pressure on her.

He mingled with the crowd, making sure everyone
was happy and had a drink in their hand. Everyone
complimented him on a fine establishment and told
him how great the night was and how much fun they
were having.

He was outside in the beer garden delivering a
round of cocktails to a table of young women when he
felt a tap on his back. He turned to see Scarlett
standing there. She was dressed in a floral summer
dress with sandals on her feet and her hair swept back
in her usual bun. Her neck was bare and beckoned him

to touch it with his lips, to discover all the dips and crevices of her body. But New Year's wasn't a night for one-night stands . . . so why was his body acting like this?

"You came." Even to his own ears, his voice came across as husky.

She lowered her long, dark lashes. "I said I would."

Yes, she had, but he still hadn't wanted to get his hopes up. But there she was. In the flesh. A very beautiful flesh package, too. Her skin looked more bronze than usual in the glimmering outdoor lights, and he wondered if she had been spending some more time outside. The glow suited her.

Aware that his jeans suddenly felt a size too small, Linc tore his gaze away and shifted his weight to his other leg.

"This place looks amazing." She looked around, and his eyes followed her gaze. It really was a great turnout. Exactly how he had planned it and what he'd hoped for, right down to the twinkling lights dangling above them.

"Thank you. I'm really glad you came."

"Me too." Her voice was a whisper, and he almost lost it on the breeze.

"Let's get you a drink." He offered her his hand, and she only looked at it for a second before placing hers in it. He led her through the bustling crowds of people until they reached the bar. There, he beckoned her to take the only free seat as he made his way to the other side of the the wooden countertop. Once they were face-to-face again, he asked for her order.

"What do you recommend?"

"Hmm. Do you like fruity drinks?" he asked.

She nodded, a slow smile forming.

"Do you like strawberries?"

She nodded again, much more enthusiastically this time.

He grabbed a glass and started pouring from the closest tap. The bartenders beside him were busy filling orders, and he made a mental note to check the supply levels. The last thing he wanted was for the taps to run empty.

When the glass was full, he placed it on a coaster in front of her. "This is my newest blend with strawberry and rhubarb flavours."

She raised her eyebrows, and he watched as she first smelt the drink, then took the tiniest sip. "It's really good."

"Are you sure? You barely tasted it."

Something flitted across her face, almost like she was arguing with herself. "I don't really drink, so when I do, I have to take it very slowly."

"Ah. A lightweight." Not surprising, really, given the size of her. He'd bet she barely ate a thing, too.

He poured himself a water and then leaned across the bar, chatting with her for a while. The conversation came so easily between them. She continued to sip the beer slowly and Linc finished his water. He wasn't drinking tonight, even though many of his friends had wanted to toast his success. He had to set the example for his staff and keep a clear head.

Lilly sidled up next to Scarlett. He recognised the dance teacher from the pub and also from the concert. If he remembered correctly, she had been tap dancing on the stage.

"Hi, Linc." She offered him a wave. "Congratulations. This place is fantastic."

"Thanks. I'm glad you're having fun. Do you need a top-up?" He pointed at her empty glass.

"Yes, please." Lilly gave him her order, and he busied himself fixing her drinks. From the corner of his eye, he could see the two women chatting. Each of them would occasionally glance at him as though he was their topic of conversation.

If they were, he hoped they were saying good things.

Just as he was finishing the last glass, one of the staff members approached and told him they'd run out of tonic water.

He placed the drinks in front of Lilly, then turned to Scarlett. "I have to go do something. I'll catch up with you later?"

"No problem." She smiled reassuringly at him, and he had to forcibly tear himself away from her.

Once he'd refilled the taps and dealt with all the other issues that needed his attention, he looked at his watch. It was already approaching midnight. The crowds were still bustling, the beer still flowing, and no one seemed to have any intention of leaving until after the New Year had been rung in. The TV monitors were playing the national coverage of the festivities happening in Sydney. At midnight, the fireworks display would start on the iconic Sydney Harbour Bridge. They wouldn't get to see it live since Queensland wasn't on Daylight Savings Time like the rest of the east coast, but it would be played at midnight for the state's benefit.

He made his rounds through the patrons, collecting empty glasses and cans and chatting, making sure everyone was enjoying themselves. All the time, he kept an eye out for Scarlett.

People stared at him, women especially, and normally he took it in his stride, but something about Scarlett Matthews' gaze, the way her lips parted as she slowly raked the length of his body, made him tense.

She had been talking to Hamish Pearson, the owner of the local coffee roastery, Maleny Roast'd, when their eyes met through the crowded room. He let his gaze linger. She was so beautiful in that soft pink flowery dress. He ached to touch that glowing skin and see if it was as soft as it looked.

And those full, pouty, pink lips.

When he'd made his way over to them, he shook Hamish's hand. The men had been close friends for years, both entering entrepreneurship at the same time with their chosen beverages.

"I'm so happy for you, mate." Hamish smiled broadly at him. "Greer sends her apologies that she couldn't come. She's home with the baby." Fatherhood suited Hamish. He and Greer had started rather untraditionally by getting pregnant and then falling in love, but they were embracing their life together and were a beautiful family now with their son, Caleb.

It almost made Linc want a family of his own. But that would mean giving up his freedom and having to be responsible for someone else.

"No worries. I'm glad you could come," Linc said and turned to Scarlett. "Do you two know each other?"

"Audrey introduced us." Scarlett had to speak loudly over the crowds. "Hamish has been telling me how important Sunshine Brew is to the town and how much you give back to the community."

Linc normally brushed off those types of compliments. Most people in Maleny gave what they could to their community by way of financial donations or by volunteering in one of the various groups or events. As a member of the APEX committee, Linc and the other blokes were often found manning the barbecues at local soccer games and at the annual country show.

His skin heated, and he hoped the redness in his cheeks wasn't too obvious in the low lighting. "We all pitch in when we can."

"Speaking of which," said Hamish, "are you still on for the charity golf game next weekend?"

Linc grinned. Apart from beer and women, his

other great passion was golf, and the Maleny Golf Club had designed a very good course which meandered through bushland and over hilly terrain, making for an eventful round.

"Of course. I've already paid for our tickets," he said.

Someone turned the TV up and everyone turned to see the countdown start.

Linc moved ever so slightly closer to Scarlett as the excited buzz of the room wrapped around them.

"Five, four, three ..."

Linc turned to look at Scarlett. Should he try to kiss her? What about his rule never to start a new year with a woman he didn't intend to finish it with?

Wait, did he maybe want to finish it with her? What the fuck?

"Two, one. Happy New Year!" The crowd whooped and shouted around them.

Scarlett was watching him, their faces only a few inches apart.

When her plump, pink lips parted, he lost all control, and his mouth pressed against hers. It took all his strength not to deepen the kiss—not to feed from her lips and explore that luscious mouth. He let his lips linger for just a moment longer than etiquette would deem appropriate, then withdrew slowly, searching her eyes for any sign of regret.

He saw none—only a glimmer of something. Disappointment?

Before he could think more about it, they were

caught in the celebrations of the crowd. "Happy New Year's," was said to each other, and hugs and handshakes were exchanged by everyone around them.

Then he was being pulled away from Scarlett, but he held her gaze as long as he could as his friends swept him away.

Hamish was the first person to call it quits for the night, and it quickly became an exodus after that as people registered how late it had gotten. They had seen in the New Year—now it was time to head home and make the most of the following public holiday.

Scarlett lingered by the bar, unsure if she should wait around but eager to get a last glance at Linc before the magical night came to an end.

She had seen a different side of Linc tonight. He had been friendly with everyone, making them all feel welcome and special. The bar was certainly a place people would want to come back to time and time again.

The way people had spoken of him—how generous he was with his time and money, always seeking to help the community—had made her see him in a new light. He might have been a player, but from all accounts, he wasn't hurting anyone with his lifestyle. The hook-ups were consensual good fun. And what was so wrong with that? Men and women had needs.

Itches that needed to be scratched from time to time. It had been a while since Scarlett had had that itch scratched. And with all that experience, Linc was probably very good at it.

A shock of lust barrelled through her system as she thought of how he might touch and tease her. Her senses said *yes* as much as her head said *no*. She didn't need to be a rocket scientist to know that Linc touching her was a bad idea. When had a casual fling ever been enough for her?

She'd had a total of one lover and that had been a drawn-out episode of neglect and mistreatment. He had only been with her because of her position in the company, not for who she was as a person. She didn't know how to be in a normal relationship, let alone play out a casual fling with a man she would then have to see at community events.

Audrey and Wes waved as they headed for the exit. She watched as they parted the crowd and found Linc in a corner of the room where Scarlett hadn't seen him. He pulled his attention away from whoever he was talking to—she couldn't see them—to say goodbye to his friends.

He remained in her line of sight after they left. As more people left, she could see who he was talking to.

A young woman with long brown hair, short denim shorts, and a tight black singlet was engaging in what could only be interpreted as flirting. She was touching his arm, laughing prettily, and playing with her hair.

Linc's back was to Scarlett so she couldn't see his reaction, but she'd bet he was loving it. Flirting right back and lining her up for a fun night in his bed.

The jealousy that swept through her caught her off-guard. Scarlett had no claim on the ginger-haired man. He had made no promises or commitments to her. She had rejected his attentions and dismissed him, so what right did she have now?

She was preparing herself to look away and leave when Linc raised both arms, placed them on the girl's arms and removed her hand from his bicep.

The disappointed look on the girl's face almost made Scarlett feel sorry for her.

Almost.

Then Linc turned and their eyes met. That delicious squirming of desire slivered all the way down to her toes. He looked at her like she was the only person in the room. Like she was the only woman he was interested in.

The feeling both empowered and scared her.

Even considering doing anything with Linc was a bad idea. He was a man who got what he wanted, and she could not risk her heart again—no matter how much she wanted to.

With that thought ringing loudly in her head, Scarlett turned on her heel and rushed out of the bar. She needed to put some distance between them and hope he soon forgot all about her.

CHAPTER 5

"*A*re you setting any New Year's resolutions?" Audrey asked over a cup of coffee.

Meredith's Cafe was a local favourite, with its green plants, eclectic framed pictures and quotes on the walls. Scarlett loved the boho vibe and their locally roasted coffee was delicious.

"No, I don't believe in resolutions. Just goals," she admitted to her friend. She had always had lofty goals in the company. Become a soloist. Dance the lead in *Giselle.*

Goals had steps you could break down and work toward. Not like resolutions that people made on New Year's Eve and forgot about the next morning.

Although her decision not to see Linc again was so far working out. Here it was, three days after the bar had opened, and she hadn't seen him around town.

"So, no desire run a marathon, give up gluten or fall in love?" Audrey prodded.

"No way," Scarlett replied, a little too emphatically. "Love is off the agenda for me. This year and forever."

Audrey leaned across the table and spoke quietly, "Why are you so against falling in love? You could be so happy."

"I am happy. I have a job I love, I get to live in this beautiful town, and I have friends like you to keep me company if I get lonely."

"But don't you miss it?"

Scarlett furrowed her brows. "Miss what?"

A cheeky smile spread over Audrey's face. "Sex."

Scarlett couldn't help the blush that warmed her cheeks. Blame her conservative childhood, but that kind of conversation still embarrassed her. Sex had certainly taken a back seat while she was dancing. Her focus had always been on ballet first, boys second. Her teenage nickname, Queen Bun-Head, had been well earned.

Scarlett concentrated her attention on the napkin her fingers were slowly shredding into tiny pieces. "No."

"Really? You don't miss being touched and plea-sured by someone? A good bed session could help release all that tension so tightly bound up in you."

"What tension? I'm more relaxed now than I ever have been."

Audrey stared at her with eyes wide open. "Now I'm

wishing I'd gotten you a massage voucher for Christmas."

Scarlett laughed. Was her friend right? Was she just fooling herself about being relaxed?

"Linc is really into you. I could tell at the bar. Perhaps getting a guy like him into bed is exactly what you need."

"That will make me more relaxed?"

"It could help you to move on. If you can see that it's not a big deal to the other person, then maybe it won't be such a big deal to you."

"Sex as therapy?" Scarlett tilted her head. "Is that a thing?"

"No idea." Audrey took a big gulp from her latte. "What's the worst it can do? You have a little no-strings fun, enjoy yourself, and if you're still having issues then I'll definitely get you a voucher for a massage. A whole bunch of them."

Sex as therapy seemed like a much more enjoyable way to deal with her tension than a massage—not to mention it wouldn't send her broke.

Audrey emptied her mug and pushed back her chair. "And here's your chance. Linc just walked in."

Scarlett's pulse quickened as she turned to look over her shoulder.

Never had a pair of khaki tradie's duds looked so good. It wasn't just Linc's long legs—it was the snug fit. The heavy fabric curved around his thighs and bum like a second skin, with stretchy inserts at the knees and hips, and pockets with flaps that opened invitingly. The eye candy didn't end there either. His V-neck shirt sat flush against his chest, outlining its breadth and the muscles beneath, and it highlighted the contrast between his trim belly and powerful shoulders.

"Keep Scarlett company for me, would you?" Audrey said to Linc as she pulled her vacant chair out for him. After throwing a cheeky smile at her friend, she hurried off.

Linc looked between Audrey's disappearing frame and Scarlett. His eyebrow raised he looked at her. Scarlett melted under his gaze, those eyes that seemed to look into her very soul.

When she still didn't speak, he pulled out the chair and sat. His knee bumped gently against hers. "I was hoping to run into you again."

"Why?" She didn't mean to sound blunt. *Be cool.* Why did she let him affect her this way?

"You left the party the other night without saying goodbye."

"Sorry about that. You seemed a bit preoccupied."

"It was a really busy night." He leaned forward on his elbows. "How about I make it up to you?"

Her heart thumped loudly in her ears. "You don't have to do that."

"No, I'd like to. Could I take you out for dinner?" His voice was a deep whisper now—quiet enough that she had to lean in closer to hear him. "Just the two of us."

Gulp. She tried to remember all those reasons she didn't want to get involved with Linc. She knew they were good reasons but right then, none of them were coming to mind.

"Okay," she replied.

She was rewarded with a smile more genuine than she had ever seen on Linc before. It gave her a tiny thread of hope that maybe she had been wrong. Maybe it would be worth hanging out with Linc and seeing where things went.

Before she could change her mind, he whipped out his phone and asked for her number and address. She gave them to him and agreed to be picked up at seven that night.

"I'll see you tonight then," he said. "I'm really looking forward to it."

"Me too," she replied as he stood and put his phone back in his pocket.

"See you then." He turned and walked out, leaving Scarlett alone to mull over what had just happened and why she was drawn to this man who was so obviously wrong for her.

Right on time, there was a knock at her door. Scarlett rose from the couch, where she had been nervously sitting, preparing herself for the night ahead.

Linc only wanted a one-night stand. She repeated the sentence to herself over and over again as she slicked on some lip gloss. That was all she wanted too. Sex as therapy, remember? Sure, dinner wasn't necessarily part of the plan, but it'd be nice to spend a little time with him before they jumped into bed. All she had to do was spend time with him, let him touch her with those hands that made her sizzle, and then leave without falling for him. Simple.

Because falling in love ends badly ...

It did, but that didn't matter, as this was very much just a one-and-done deal. No love allowed.

She let out a deep breath before putting on a smile and opening the door.

A smile curved the edges of his mouth as she took him in. His chin was clean-shaven, his short hair slightly damp. His close-fitting faded denim jeans moulded over strong-looking thighs. He wore a black dress shirt with the sleeves loosely rolled, exposing muscled forearms with gold hairs. As she breathed in, she caught an enticing waft of citrus and scrubbed healthy male. She couldn't drag her eyes away from him.

Perhaps catching her intense appraisal, he gave her a cheeky wink. She glanced away, embarrassed by her blatant ogling and flustered by her body's reaction to him.

"Hi." She finally managed to get a word out of her mouth.

"Evening, Scarlett. You look amazing tonight." His eyes travelled the length of her body.

Earlier, she had pulled everything out of her wardrobe and tried multiple outfits on. Looking at herself in the full-length mirror, she hadn't liked anything on her. All her pants made her thighs look huge and her dresses were too revealing. In the end, she had opted for a white cotton dress which scooped low down her chest but kept her shoulders covered.

"Do you like Thai food?" he asked.

She nodded without thinking, knowing she would go to McDonald's with him if that was what he'd suggested, calories be damned.

"Great. The Thai here is the best on the Sunshine Coast, and it's got a great view too." He moved to let her pass him and lock the door before she followed him to his car.

They drove through the night, the streetlights twinkling like stars in the growing darkness. Scarlett relaxed and let the motion of the drive wash over her, soothing her as the engine hummed.

Soon they arrived at their destination, the smell of exotic spices and delicious food wafting out as they stepped inside.

They were shown to a table next to a three-tier fountain. Water was pumped up from a bowl the Budda statue was holding. The tinkling sound of the water journeying down the statue made for a serene background noise.

"This is such a great spot," Scarlett said, gazing out the window where the hills declined and revealed the sparkling lights of Maroochydore below.

"I'm glad you like it." Linc's voice was gentle and soft. "The Pad Thai is my favourite dish."

"Oh yum. I haven't had Pad Thai in …" Her voice floated away as she tried to remember her last meal that hadn't been a salad.

Scarlett chose the Thai Beef Salad while Linc ordered the Chicken Pad Thai. Then they sipped on their drinks as they chatted. Their conversation consisted of safe small talk before Linc leaned in and asked her to tell him more about her career as a dancer.

"I trained in ballet my whole life and have wanted to be a professional ballerina ever since I was eight years old."

"Then why did you quit?"

"I retired. I got too old." The word tasted dirty in her mouth. She would never have stopped dancing if her body had been able to keep up. That was the reason she'd stopped. Well, that and her boyfriend dumping her for a replacement. A young, shiny, new dancer with perfect feet and a stunning face.

"You must have had lots of amazing experiences. What was your favourite moment?"

"It was my first lead role, a small classical ballet, but it was a sign...a sign that my career was going in the right direction. A sign that maybe I could make it all the way to principal.'

"I wish I could have seen it. I bet you looked amazing." The quiet certainty in Linc's voice shot a bolt of pure electricity through Scarlett's veins. "You certainly did at the Christmas show." His voice became low and husky, enveloping her like a warm blanket.

"I used to be able to pirouette seven, sometimes eight times. Now I'm lucky to do four." The dizzying rush of the move flashed before her. The audience whirring past her as she kept up speed, turning gracefully on one pointed foot. Her toes painfully straining against her shoe. Humans weren't designed to do such moves and as a result, ballerinas often suffered all sorts of foot and ankle problems. Scarlett was no exception. She sometimes thought it was dancers like her who kept the painkiller producers in business. There was a time she had lived on them.

The waitress returned to them with dishes and a plate of Spring Rolls. Scarlett hoped Linc was hungry as she knew she would barely make a dent on hers. It smelled so delicious though. The Thai aromas lingered tantalisingly in the air.

"So, why Maleny?" Linc asked as he reached for a spring roll and crunched into it. Scarlett watched as he chewed, those delicious lips devouring the delicious food. It sent warmth to the juncture between her legs. It had been years since she had desired a man's touch. His body.

"Um …" She shook her head, forcing her thoughts back to the moment. "It was Audrey. She got in touch with me and asked if I wanted to take up teaching. We've known each other for years, and I knew she'd be a great boss. And there was nothing keeping me in Brisbane."

Lincoln very subtly pushed the bowl of Pad Thai towards her. Scarlett shook her head at the noodle dish and instead speared a tomato from her salad with her fork and raised it to her mouth. She chewed slowly, enjoying every little taste and sensation.

Forget about the calories. Easier said than done.

She felt Linc watching her, and she darted her tongue out to catch any sauce that may have remained on her lips.

He shifted in his seat opposite her before lifting his beer and taking a long drink.

Conversation flowed easily as they chatted about their lives, jobs, and friends. Scarlett relaxed into her seat and slowly picked at her food, surprised when the empty plates were cleared away by the waitstaff and dessert menus presented.

"Nothing for me," she said as she pushed the menu away. After all that delicious food, she was surprised her stomach wasn't bursting.

"Coffee then?" Linc suggested, looking at her as though he would like nothing better than to have her for dessert. The idea sent warmth and longing through her body. Arousal was a feeling she hadn't experienced in a long time. What if she was no good at sex anymore? She'd had a total of one lover, so her experience was limited, and he had never given her any feed-back or suggestions. And now, here she was, ready to bring that number of lovers to two—in just a few short minutes. Good God, was she really doing this?

She shook her head. "No, thank you."

Linc paid the bill and they walked to his car. He opened the door for her to slide in. The drive back to her house was filled with tension. Should she ask him in? Would he presume he was invited? The anxiety of the situation had Scarlett's stomach turning in knots. Was she really ready for this?

He pulled into her driveway and climbed out of the car and and opened her door. "Thanks," she whispered into the night.

"My pleasure." His voice was husky and delicious. He gently took her hand in his as they walked to her front door. Then, when she turned to him to make up an excuse for her nerves, he leaned in and captured her lips with his.

Her lips were just as soft as he'd expected, and she tasted like strawberry ChapStick. Her mouth had been teasing him all night, every time she had opened it to eat or talk, and that tongue when she licked her lips! Oh, he almost groaned thinking about it. He made sure to keep the kiss gentle. He needed to take it slowly with Scarlett. She was too fragile and easily scared away.

He was readying himself to end the kiss when she opened her lips, and she was kissing him back—seeming as lost to the moment as he was while their tongues intertwined in a sensual dance, and he felt every last synapse in his body come screaming to life. Wanting her. Wanting more.

He pulled her against his chest and wrapped his arms around her back. She fit perfectly against him. Like their bodies had been made for each other.

Slow down! He heard his brain demand it. He stepped back. Scarlett looked dazed, her skin flushed and her eyes still half-closed. It was the sexiest thing he'd ever seen.

"Do you want to come inside?" she whispered.

His body screamed *yes* but his brain took back control. "Thank you for a lovely evening." He thrust his hands in his pockets, turned, and practically ran back to his car. He had to leave quickly before he changed his mind.

Shame crashed through him as he glanced back at her and saw the hurt on her face.

Damn.

Some people were made for togetherness, and some people were just an emotional ticking time bomb—set to detonate and destroy everything in their path. Linc knew which he was and he wasn't about to throw that grenade into anyone's life.

CHAPTER 6

When Scarlett awoke the next morning, instead of jumping out of bed and doing pilates, she snuggled back under the doona, cringing at the memory of Linc's rejection.

She had totally misunderstood that Linc was just giving her a cursory, end-of-date kiss goodnight and she had not only matched his kiss but asked him to do more.

She'd been deep in the most sensual, bone-melting kiss of her life, aching, needing more, and then he had stopped.

What was the matter with her? What had she done wrong? Was she not sexy enough? Had she been too easy? Wasn't that what he wanted though? Just sex? She had been a willing partner—had that not been obvious?

Her phone buzzed on the bedside table and she blindly reached for it. Bringing her mobile under the covers, she saw a message from Audrey, asking if she wanted to join her at the gym.

Scarlett wavered between staying in bed all day and falling deeper into depression or getting up and working off last night's meal.

She typed out a reply, saying she'd be there soon, then threw off the sheets and forced her feet to hit the floor. She pushed all thoughts of Linc from her mind as she dressed in her favourite purple workout clothes and laced up her sneakers. In the kitchen, she blended a protein smoothie and took her vitamins. She felt better already.

After grabbing her gym bag, which was always packed and ready to go, she locked the door behind her and started walking up the street to the gym.

People would be strolling around the Sunday market on Maple Street now, buying their weekly fruit and vegetables. Perhaps she would stop there on her way home and see what was on offer.

As she rounded the corner, she saw Audrey heading in her direction. She waved as her friend jogged to meet up with her.

"So? I want all the details." They continued walking together.

Damn, Scarlett thought, why had she let slip to Audrey about her date with Linc? Now she would have to relive the embarrassment all over again.

She did her best to shrug it off. "It was fine, but I don't think he's that into me."

Audrey frowned. "What makes you say that?"

"We were having a great time, and when he dropped me off we …"

Audrey stopped walking and turned to face her. "You what?"

Scarlett's cheeks burned. "We kissed."

A huge grin spread across Audrey's lovely face.

"Then he pulled back and practically sprinted away."

Scarlett could practically hear Audrey's thoughts ticking over as a range of expressions crossed her face.

"He didn't try to sleep with you?"

Scarlett shook her head. "And trust me, it wouldn't have been a hard deal to seal."

"So you had a great date and he kissed you good night and then left?"

Scarlett nodded.

"Wow, he must really like you!"

Scarlett held up her hands. "Because he didn't want to sleep with me?"

"Exactly!" Audrey exclaimed as they started walking again. "He's never done that before because he's never really liked anyone before."

Scarlett laughed. "That's ridiculous!"

"Linc is a complicated person. Who isn't?"

Scarlett pondered her friend's words as they entered the gym. She needed to burn off some unspent energy and decide just what to do about Linc now.

CHAPTER 7

*L*incoln had already been on the golf course for an hour. He found the peace on the green relaxing, almost meditative. Alone with his thoughts, he could practise his swing and try not to think about the way he had left things with Scarlett.

He should forget about her. Nothing good could come from him trying to have a normal relationship. He didn't do relationships. He'd never even gone out with somebody for more than a week. He had long ago realised that commitment, marriage, and kids were not in the cards for this long-term bachelor.

But if anyone could change his mind, it would be Scarlett. The ballet dancer with her perfect pointe and pouty lips would be able to soften even the hardest man's resolve. But a relationship wouldn't be fair to her, would it? Not with his crazy hours and independent customs. She would be much better off with a man who wasn't so set in his ways. Someone who truly wanted that happily ever after life.

He glanced at the time on his phone. Hamish was meant to be joining him, but, as usual had been held up by the baby. As cute as Caleb was, he had turned his friend's life upside down. Now instead of big nights out, drinking and partying, Hamish was home for dinner and bath time without fail.

And Hamish had never been happier. The complete love and adoration showed on his face and echoed in his voice whenever he spoke of his new little family.

But that didn't mean that lifestyle was right for everyone.

Lincoln loved his niece. But he also loved his lifestyle just the way it was, and he didn't think a girlfriend would improve it.

He lined up another ball and swung his club, sending the ball to soar and land exactly where Lincoln had aimed.

He replaced his club and pulled his golf bag behind him as he walked to the green. The breeze on the hill was a nice change from the humidity that had been hanging around. A cluster of puffy white clouds drifted across the sky.

He loved Maleny. The rolling green hills, the huge Bunya trees, and the friendly small-town community. Even as an ambitious young entrepreneur, he had never felt the need to leave the town he had been born and raised in. He loved that many of his friends were farmers or lived off the land. They all wanted to give back to the community that had given so much to them.

Caught up in his thoughts, he didn't see Hamish approaching until his friend was practically right beside him.

"Sorry I'm late," Hamish said as he wheeled his golf bag over. "Caleb had a rough night."

"No worries," Lincoln replied, happy his friend was there to distract him from his thoughts.

They played and chatted for a few holes, enjoying the morning before Hamish finally brought up Scarlett's name.

"Heard you took her for Thai."

"How did you hear that?" Linc shot him a look. "No wait—don't tell me."

Linc could guess. Greer, Hamish's wife, was an esteemed chef, having worked at fine restaurants around the world before coming home to her family dairy farm, Emerald Hills. She and her sister Freya had built a restaurant on the property and ran farm tours. It had become one of the most popular attractions in the Hinterland.

"Do you forget how small a town this is? Greer knows all the other chefs in town and is also friends with the owners. Not to mention her cousin's daughter just started waiting tables there," Hamish said.

Linc sighed, remembering his date with Scarlett— the easy conversation and the obvious chemistry they shared. She was everything he could want in a woman. She was warm, caring, generous, loving, and passionate. Any man would be lucky to be with her.

"Just my personal opinion, mate," Hamish said, "but I think you two would make a great couple. Plus I'd really like to see you try having a relationship. You don't know what you're missing."

Linc pondered his friend's words as they teed off at the start of a new hole. Maybe he should give them a chance. Another date wouldn't be the worst thing after all. They could take it really slowly, get to know each other better and see if they really were a good fit or not.

That was if he hadn't already ruined his chances. He pulled out his phone and sent her a quick text, thanking her for last night and asking if she would like to catch up for a coffee soon.

The blinking ellipses appeared on his mobile screen, indicating she was typing a reply. Then, after a minute or so, they disappeared. He refreshed the screen just to be sure, but there was no new message.

Shit. I really might have blown my chance.

"Come on, slow coach," Hamish called from farther up the path and waved for him to catch up. Linc slid his phone in his back pocket, readjusted his grip on his golf bag, and followed his friend to find their balls. If he had ruined his chance with Scarlett, then maybe there was no changing her mind.

Then again, maybe there was something he could do to make up for it.

Scarlett dismissed her senior students and walked over to get her water bottle from the table. She took a deep drink before waking up her phone. There was a message from Linc—the first in two days.

She read his apology for the way he left things after their date. He wanted to make it up to her.

Scarlett had spent the last two days trying not to think about Linc, keeping busy with classes and exercising even more often. She had even gone to her first yoga class this morning and had found it surprisingly calming. Chloe, the teacher, had been lovely and welcoming. The beginners' class had been a small group of mostly older women, but Chloe had talked them through each pose and shown them how to modify it for their ability. At the end, they had laid down on their mats in Savasana and relaxed to gentle meditation music. When Scarlett had come up from the position she had felt more energised and positive—ready to face the day.

Before leaving, she'd had a long talk to Chloe and booked in for regular sessions.

Scarlett rolled her head and shoulders as her next group of students skipped into the studio. She wasn't quite ready to deal with Linc just yet.

Linc stared through the glass window pane at the frozen vegetables in the supermarket. The cool air blowing against him was refreshing after the humid warmth of the day outside. What was he looking for? He rubbed his palm over his face, his brain still clouded with thoughts of Scarlett and how, after almost a week and several texts, she still hadn't responded to him. He would have to accept the fact that he was being ghosted —an experience that was entirely new to him. Instead of focusing on it, he had thrown himself into work. Since the opening, he had been kept busy with book-ings, and everyone was raving about how great the place was. Write-ups in the local papers and on social media had all been positive, and people were even coming up the Sunshine Coast just to visit. He should be focusing on his success, but he really just wanted to share it with Scarlett. To see her lovely smile.

He grabbed a bag of frozen fries from the freezer and closed the door, watching as it instantly fogged over. Putting the bag in his trolly, he turned his gaze forward and started pushing. He wanted to be finished the shopping so he could finally go home, have a quick meal, and get some sleep.

He sensed her presence before he saw her.

With a shopping basket in one hand, she was dressed in three-quarter-length black leggings and a light blue T-shirt which was tied at the waist. The smallest glimmer of white skin showed which, of course, was the first thing he saw. His blood pulsed harder through his body as his hands ached to touch her. To see if her skin was as pale everywhere on her body as it was around her hips

She stopped walking as their eyes met across the aisle.

"Hi," she finally said. "How are you?"

"Yeah, good. And you?" He hated how awkward he sounded.

"Busy." She shrugged and took a tentative step, clearly eager to flee at the first opening.

"I, ah, wanted to say sorry for the other day." He rushed his words, wanting to get them out before anyone overheard him and they became the number-one topic of community gossip. "I'm sorry I left so quickly. It was rude of me."

Her eyes rounded. "It was rather abrupt. I thought I'd done something wrong.

He left his trolly and moved closer to her. He caught a whiff of her floral-scented body spray and almost lost control. "You didn't do anything wrong. I didn't want to rush things with you. I wanted to take it slow and didn't trust myself to do that."

"Really?" Her grey eyes looked deeply into his, and he felt like she could see right into his soul. Vulnerability was not one of his strong points, and he knew it would take some effort to break down those well-built walls.

"I'd really like to take you out again." His voice was hoarse and quiet.

She took her time before answering with a nod. "Okay."

His heart lifted in his chest. "Great. I'll, um, text you and set something up."

She smiled, presumably at his sudden awkwardness.

"I'll look forward to it," she replied before moving past him to continue down the aisle. He turned and watched her go. Her long legs and perfect bottom provided some very nice entertainment.

He would have to think of something really good for their next date

He didn't want to screw this chance up again.

CHAPTER 8

*I*t was a sticky, hot day when Linc picked Scarlett up and drove her the short distance to Gardners Falls. He parked as close to the falls as he could, although, judging from the cars, it would be a popular spot today. Apart from the school pool in town, this was the only spot to swim during the warm summer months.

Linc gathered the Esky and bag from the car and led Scarlett down to the waterhole.

"Oh, wow," she exclaimed as the river came in to view. The current was gentle and the water almost perfectly clear as it weaved around rocks. Vegetation grew on the high cliffs beyond.

Linc smiled as he walked to his favourite spot under a gum tree and set up the rug. Scarlett settled herself on it and continued to take in the surroundings.

Families and children of all ages splashed in the

shallow rock pools while the teenagers jumped into the deeper pool and and threw footballs to each other.

Linc waved as some people he knew walked past. It wasn't the most private of spots, but he wasn't trying to hide his relationship with Scarlett or his feelings for her.

"This is so great," she said, turning to him. "Thank you for bringing me here."

He lay on his side, propped up on his elbow, and smiled at her. "You're welcome. We used to come here all the time as kids. We'd ride our bikes through the farms and stay here all day." He thought again how lucky he had been to grow up with such a childhood.

"That sounds amazing," she replied, lying down on her side too. "I spent my childhood inside, dancing or working out."

"But look where it got you." He pretended to push some hair off her face, but really he just wanted to touch her. "You achieved all those dreams and goals you set for yourself."

"True"—she nodded—"but I missed out on a lot too."

"Well, there is plenty of time to make up for that now. How about a swim?"

She smiled widely at him

A few minutes later they had shed their clothes down to their swimsuits and were entering the water, hand in hand.

The chilly water did nothing to dampen the heat

pooling in Linc's loins as they entered the water and swam deeper until they could only just touch the rocky ground beneath. Scarlett's head bobbed as she paddled around, her hair tied up in the bun which Linc had become accustomed to now.

"This way." He waved before breast-stroking out to deeper water. The crowds lessened there and he turned, finding the cave-like hole he'd been looking for empty.

"Come sit. There's a ledge just here." He pulled himself onto it and watched as she swam over to join him.

The ledge wasn't very wide, so their legs touched and the water lapped chest-height, encouraging Linc to watch as it splashed against her breasts. Damn, she was beautiful.

"Thank you for bringing me here." She grinned at him, a playfulness in her eyes he had not seen before. Her life must always have been so serious. So planned out.

"It's nice to just take a beat and enjoy the moment." He gathered her hand in his and entwined her fingers with his own. She looked at him and opened her mouth the slightest bit as though she were about to say something.

Her lips were so full and pink. He remembered how perfect they were for kissing. His gaze flickered to her eyes, silently asking permission. When she didn't move away, he slowly moved his head closer until their lips made contact. It was a brief, gentle kiss which left him wanting more. So much more.

But he wouldn't take more until he was sure she was ready. Until he was invited.

So he slipped off the ledge and ducked under the water. His hair was dripping wet when he resurfaced. She laughed and followed him.

They found a spot in the deep pool near the water-fall. The rush of the water drowned out the noise of everyone else. They laughed as they splashed and dived around each other. Linc took every possible opportunity to touch and kiss Scarlett, and she was more than receptive to it.

Surfacing from a dive, she wiped water from her face and swam towards him slowly. He opened his arms as she moved up against him, the front of their bodies touching almost everywhere. Her arms snaked around his neck and her lips closed on his.

He tasted her lips, the fresh water making them slick and supple. His hands explored the nakedness of her back where the one-piece suit dipped low. He parted her lips and sank his tongue deeper into her mouth, stroking against hers in a sensual dance that set the world on fire.

Desire flamed through him. He had never wanted a woman so much before. He was sure that if he didn't have her soon he would explode.

The loud laughter from a group of youths had them reluctantly pulling away. That was a little embarrassing. He watched Scarlett's expression. Was she feeling the same way he was? Did she ache for him as he ached for her?

He didn't know what kind of a spell he was under, but he loved it.

Scarlett stretched lazily and repositioned her head on Linc's chest. Spread out on the blanket, basking in the sun, she couldn't think of anywhere she would rather be. She wasn't sure what had just happened between her and Linc, but whatever it was, no amount of ground rules were going to keep her safe.

Linc's sculpted chest was the perfect pillow, and his muscled arms and firm fingers seemed to know exactly where and how to touch her. The heat pooling between her thighs was getting harder and harder to ignore.

His stomach rumbled, and she laughed at its tune. "We should get you something to eat," she said.

"I know what I'd like a bite of," Linc said as he manoeuvred to nibble on her neck. She giggled.

He claimed her mouth once more, his greedy tongue begging for more.

Reluctantly, she pulled away. "Come on then. Food time." She stood, all too aware of his gaze on her as she reached for a towel.

After they packed up and walked back to the car, Linc drove them into town. It was late afternoon and the cafés had already closed up. Above them the clouds were darkening, but that did nothing to affect Scarlett's happy mood.

"Gelato shop is open," he suggested.

"Yum." She swallowed down the voice that said *don't you dare.*

They parked and walked over to the freezer, which displayed tubs and tubs of flavours of ice cream. All were made in Maleny using produce from the local dairies.

"The Cherry Ripe is my favourite," Linc whispered into her ear.

"How do you choose?"

"Go with your gut. What looks good?"

She stared into the freezer until her gaze stopped on the one thing she had never been allowed to try. "Nutella."

The server scooped the rich dark ice cream into a cone and passed it over. Linc paid and took his own cone before following her to a bench to sit and eat.

"I ..." Scarlett opened her mouth to thank him, but at that moment, a drip of gelato melted down the cone and rolled onto her wrist. Without thinking, she lifted her hand to her mouth to lick it off. She stopped dead, feeling the cool sensation slide down her throat, tasting the dense, nutty sweetness of the hazelnut, rich and delicious—an explosion of pleasure on her tongue.

She took another lick and moaned out loud. "God, this is so good!" She devoured the gelato, savouring the sweetness and creamy coolness. She looked up. Linc was watching her hungrily—an expression that had nothing to do with food.

Then, that all too familiar feeling started to twist her stomach and constrict her throat. Trying to stay calm, she slowed and deepened her breaths.

It was crazy, she knew, freaking out over one tiny ice cream, but she couldn't help it. She'd spent years counting every precious morsel she would allow between her lips, calculating calories and fat units, knowing that the slightest slip-up would edge her further and further away from her goal weight.

"Are you okay?" Linc placed a gentle hand on her shoulder.

Scarlett squeezed her eyes closed for a second then turned her attention to Linc's concerned face. The genuine worry in his eyes helped smother the flames of her anxiety.

"I'm fine. Sorry, but I'm not going to be able to finish this." She held out the ice cream cone.

"Let me get rid of it." He took the cone to the bin then quickly returned to her side. She stood up, expecting to walk, but instead he gathered her into his arms.

The tension drained from her body as she melted into his embrace. Tears burned her eyes but didn't flow. She pushed those feelings back into the box where they usually lived and concentrated on being in the moment.

It felt so good, Linc being moulded against her like that. It was warm and cosy. And he was being supportive. She had never truly had support from anyone.

She closed her eyes and raised her face, unspeaking but asking for his kiss. He happily responded with soft, reassuring lips.

Safe and secure in his embrace, she wished their kiss would never end. The anxiety in her stomach was replaced by desire and heat. She wanted more of Linc. She wanted to know every curve and muscle of his body.

As if sensing her need, he lifted his lips to ask, "Can I take you home?"

She nodded and smiled at him, her heart pounding wildly in her chest. She wanted nothing more than to be touched and enjoyed by this man.

He found her hand and held it firmly as they walked back to the car where he opened the passenger door for her and closed it once she was safely inside.

The drive back to her place seemed to last an eternity. Heated tension sizzled like fire between them. When they finally pulled up in front of Scarlett's house, Linc turned to her.

"Are you sure about this?" he asked, his voice husky with desire. Scarlett glanced at the very pronounced bulge at the juncture of his pants and felt a dampness in her own underwear.

"I've never wanted anything more," she admitted.

He had her out of the car and to the front door so

quickly she barely felt the splattering of rain against her skin. She fumbled in her purse to find the key, finally pulling it out only to find her hand shaking so much she couldn't get it in the lock.

Linc's hand came to rest on top of hers. His warm touch instantly soothed her nerves. Their gazes met and his eyes searched her face, perhaps for any further doubt. Then he raised his hand and slid it up her neck to cradle the side of her head.

How could such a simple move feel so intimate? She relaxed into his hand and was rewarded by a kiss from his hungry lips.

He finished opening the door and they moved inside as one, their mouths never losing contact as the door was shut and her key and purse were forgotten on the floor.

"Bedroom?" he murmured against her lips, laughing when all she was capable of was waving down the hall.

Then her legs went out from under her as Linc scooped her up in his arms as though she weighed nothing. Scarlett snuggled against the curve of his neck and breathed in the musky scent of him, all manly and intoxicating.

Linc put her back on her feet in the middle of the bedroom before running his hand up her back—a slow caress, hot against her skin. Her eyes didn't leave his, but she shivered under his touch, feeling the heat, the purpose behind it as his fingers traced up his spine to the back of her neck, curling to tangle in her hair.

There was no space left between them, their bodies pressed together. She was sweaty and breathless and feeling so damn right—it was like she'd been made to be there, fitted to him, chest to chest, hip to hip.

Linc leaned closer, closer, and she caught her breath, lost in the rhythm of their bodies, the intensity of his dark eyes drawing her into him. It all felt so natural, and it was the easiest thing in the world when he closed those last precious inches between them and found her lips with his.

The kiss blazed through her like wildfire. It was overwhelming, a flood of sensation like she'd never known before setting every nerve ablaze. Her brain shut off, short-circuited by the rush of pleasure, and all her hesitance was forgotten.

He unclothed her, achingly slowly, his fingers soft against her skin. His lips followed his fingers, kissing their way over her shoulders all the way to that sensitive spot on her neck.

She was shaking on the inside. She knew he would be a practised lover, far more experienced than her, and she could only hope her nerves wouldn't show.

His breathing became ragged, and he let out a guttural groan. She loved how out of control he sounded, how desperate. She wanted him to want her, to need her as much as she needed him.

She watched with hooded eyes as he dropped to his knees in front of her. Then he was spreading her legs wide again, his expression caught somewhere between pleasure and pain. His eyes lifted to meet hers for one brief, intense moment before he leaned forward. She braced her weight back on her arms as she watched his dark head draw closer and closer. The first touch of his tongue nearly sent her over the edge. Her whole body jerked, and Linc's hands clamped on her thighs. He pressed closer, his tongue hot and wet and fast against her as he kissed her with big, greedy open-mouthed hunger.

Too quickly, she felt her climax rising inside her. She fought it, wanting to savour every last second. Linc's hands slid up the outside of her thighs to her hips and drew her closer again. She tried hard to hold out, but he was so avid, so intense …

Her back arched and her thighs trembled as she came, her hips pushing against the grip of his hands. He rode out her orgasm and kept kissing her, still hungry for more. She gasped, quivering with arousal. It was too much. He was too much. She grabbed a handful of his hair and used it to drag his head up. His gaze was unfocused, his expression distracted as he looked up at her.

Kissing him fervently, she could taste herself on his lips. She wanted to please him the way he'd so easily pleased her.

Breaking the kiss, she pushed his pants down and his magnificent manhood sprung free.. She moved to lie down on her bed. He followed, shedding the rest of his clothes on his way, and retrieving a foil packet from his wallet before joining her.

Then he was on top of her. She spread her legs and guided his erection between her thighs. The first nudge of his hardness against her made her inner muscles tighten. Then he was sliding into her, thick and long and exactly what she needed. He stroked into her once, twice, then his fingers gripped her hips and he stilled.

"Fuck, you feel so good," he said.

"So do you," she moaned back.

He hesitated briefly, then he began to move again. He kissed her as his cock stroked her, his whole body hard and focused. He filled her utterly, stretched her, and every thrust sent shivers through her. Desire tightened low in her belly for the second time. His hands tightened on her hips and he thrust deeper, harder into her. She met him thrust for thrust, tilting her hips to deepen his penetration. She felt the exact moment when he reached the end of his tether. His body slammed into hers in one final, deep stroke. He pressed his hips into hers, his mouth open on her neck. Then he exhaled in a rush that almost sounded like a sob. She forgot to breathe as the last shudders of his body tipped her over into her own climax. She tightened around him, milking the last of his orgasm, totally lost to everything but the feel of him inside her, his body around her. Her heartbeat was still pounding in her ears as Linc's hand found the back of her head. He held her close for what felt like a long time, their bodies still locked together, his face pressed into her neck.

Against her better judgement, Scarlett wished that time would stand still so she could savour her body against his.

CHAPTER 9

*S*carlett woke the following morning to the smell of coffee. She opened her eyes to see Linc placing a cup on her bedside table, another in his other hand. After ordering takeout the night before, they had spent the rest of their night in bed.

"Good morning." Linc smiled at her before coming back around the bed and snuggling in next to her.

She sat up and reached for the coffee, savouring the warming aroma.

"I wanted to make us breakfast but you have very little in you fridge."

She avoided answering by kissing him instead. She could get very used to this, waking up next to Linc.

"Last night was incredible," she murmured against his mouth.

"It was." A smile curved his lips, his breath warm on

her skin. "You are so in tune with your body. You just lose yourself to the moment."

"I'm a dancer, and we're very connected to our bodies—it's beyond words." She rested her head against her hand as she spoke. "The movement, the feeling of getting the steps just right—when the painstaking choreography fits together so perfectly, I can't even feel the individual tiny actions, just the gorgeous flow as I lose myself completely in the story and the music, falling into another world until I live and breathe and exist only as a rush of motion; powerful, focused. Free."

Linc drew lazy circles on her arm as she spoke.

"A ballet is like a winding stack of dominos: from the very first step, everything should unfold as naturally and easily as breathing. But if you miss just one step, a split second, a heartbeat in time, the whole sequence falls apart. But those moments when it all comes together ... that's when I feel it—a power like no other beating through my body, like I could take flight right there on the stage. It's a drug, a shot of pure joy, and the longer I go between hits, the more I crave it, need it, desperately fight to get back there in that perfect zone where the movements roll off my body and my feet are made of stardust, golden and bright. All the work and the criticism, the pain and insecurities, they melt away, and I finally feel whole again, like I'm the person I'm meant to be. Like I'm worthy ..." Her voice trailed off as she realised how vulnerable she had just been. What would he think of her?

But his reaction was to pull her close and kiss her forehead. "You are worthy, Scarlett. Never doubt that."

There was a reason she loved ballet enough to have made it her life. Ballet was all about rules, about precision. Those things made her comfortable. Not feelings and emotions. She preferred to push those as far away from herself as possible.

Being with Linc felt so safe—like she could finally be herself for a change and not just the person people wanted her to be. She liked him way too much. And it wasn't just a sex thing. She wanted to jump him, yes. But she wanted to make him laugh, and she wanted to talk to him, and she wanted to know and understand him. She wanted to eat gelato with him, and wear what she wanted without worrying how she looked and skip a pilates class to lie in bed with him.

Maybe she could finally step away from the barre, from the ballerina, and simply be Scarlett.

CHAPTER 10

*T*hat week was one of the happiest of Linc's life. They spent most evenings together in each other's arms. He had invited Scarlett to his house where they'd prepared meals together and taken long, luxurious soaks in his hot tub. She had opened up to him like no one ever had before and he had done the same in return. He'd lowered his guard and risked exposing his emotions. But he found it so hard to contain all the feelings that she brought out in him. He wanted so much more from his life now—he wanted passion.

After turning off the lights in the brewery, he locked up and walked down to meet Scarlett at the dance studio. He couldn't wipe the smile off his face.

He wanted to make love to her all day. Just the two of them and—whoa, whoa, whoa. Make love? Linc didn't "make love". He had sex. So what the hell was this "making love" business all about?

His steps slowed. Was he really in that deep?

The certainty of his feelings hit him. He wanted Scarlett—not just for a fling but for everything.

He let his thoughts linger there.

No feelings of terror or fear of commitment seemed to arise. Instead, happiness and optimism rose up from his chest.

He couldn't wait to see Scarlett again, to hold her hand, to touch her skin. She made him want things he had never wanted before. But that thought didn't terrify him the way it once had. Instead there was a comfort and happiness there with her.

He held open the studio door as several teenage girls in pink leotards, their hair done up in buns, passed by him, giggling loudly, pink-faced from exercise.

He peeked in the studio and saw Scarlett wiping her face with a towel. "You look like you just hit the gym hard."

She turned and her face lit up as she looked at him. "I feel a bit like it!" She moved towards him and kissed him. "How was your day?"

"It was good. Better now though." He nibbled the delicate curve of her neck.

"Ahem."

Linc looked up, startled at seeing Audrey at the door, hints of a smile showing on face.

"I'm off," Audrey said. "Are you right to lock up when you leave?"

"Yeah." Scarlett walked towards the door. "Thanks, I'll see you in the morning."

Audrey nodded. "You two have a good night." She waved and left.

Scarlett spun slowly on her heel. "Caught in the act! I'm going to have some explaining to do tomorrow." She chuckled as she moved back into Linc's arms like a magnet unable to stay away.

He kissed her again and moved her gently towards a mirrored wall. He kissed her, hungrily, and she replied with just as much need.

He pressed her up against the barre, his hands gripping the wooden rail on either side of her hips. He pressed urgently against her, and she arched into him with equal candour. She ran her hands up the sides of his thighs, skimming the tight curve of his behind until her hands reached his back.

"I don't know what I'm doing," she whispered against his mouth. "But I can't stop wanting to touch you, wanting to taste you."

His lips ran dry at her last statement, his tongue heavy in his mouth as he steadied his breath. His blood seemed to pulse twice as fast as usual as he looked at her, his flickering glance capturing the flush of her pale skin under the fluorescent lights. The arousal he'd been fighting pooled in his groin, and desire wrenched inside him.

"I've never felt this kind of attraction to anyone before," she said.

He turned his attention to her face, all wide-eyed and needy. "Funny, I was just thinking the exact same thing." He kissed her slower this time. "Can I take you home?"

She ran her hands through his hair as she replied, "Yes please."

He held her bag as she locked up the studio. Then he opened the entrance door only to be greeted with a downpour of rain. He hadn't even noticed the storm rolling in earlier and had left his car parked up the road.

"My car is just over there." She pointed a few metres away to the car park.

He nodded and took the opportunity to link his arm through hers. "I don't think the weather is going to ease anytime soon. Let's make a break for it."

"Wait." She left his side and returned a moment later with an umbrella. She opened it as he opened the door against the raging wind.

They huddled under the umbrella. Scarlett shrieked as the rain hit them head-on. They rushed down the pavement towards the car park. The ground was slippery, and he held her tight so that her body bumped against him as they sprinted.

"Quickly!" she cried. Some of her hair had escaped the bun and was whipping around her face like a series of wet ebony ribbons. He pulled her towards the second row of cars, and she fumbled with her keys. He saw her safely in the driver's side before dashing around to the passenger side.

The doors slammed loudly as they fell into the car in a rush, their breathing fogging up the windows. Scarlett's laugh was a joy to his heart; even drenched and puffing, she was a vision.

He manoeuvred himself in his seat and captured her face in his hands. He paused as he gazed upon her face. Unspoken words welled up in his throat.

He kissed her lips, certain he would never be able to get enough of her.

Scarlett fumbled with her keys before finally unlocking her front door and walking through with Linc close behind.

He glanced around the sparsely furnished lounge. Few personal touches told him anything more about Scarlett except for one small silver trophy sitting alone on a shelf. He stepped toward it so he could read the inscription.

"Best Technique," he read aloud before noticing the date. It was from almost twenty years ago. Surely she would have received so many more trophies and awards since then. "Why is this the only one you display?"

Scarlett approached and placed a single finger on

top of the trophy and gently stroked its rounded top. "This was the one that meant the most. I remember everyone was so jealous when I won it. I was finally good at something, you know? Better than anyone else in that class."

Linc watched as she seemed to retreat to that time as a little girl, then with a little shake of her head, she turned back to him and he wondered if he had just imagined it.

He raised his hand and gently stroked her soft cheek. She reminded him of one of those crystal statues his mum owned. A ballerina forever frozen in a graceful pose, balancing on one pointe shoe with the other leg straight up in the air, her arms off to the side. So beautiful, so fragile. So wounded.

He so desperately wanted to put all Scarlett's broken pieces back together for her so she would never feel pain again. Something warned him that he might be her greatest cause of pain. But he couldn't. He wouldn't.

"I'll never hurt you—I promise you that." He spoke the words aloud before tugging her head towards his and pressing his lips against hers.

All thoughts left his mind as she opened up for him and submitted to his hungry mouth. He pressed her against the wall as he pulled down one of the straps on her leotard, baring a small breast. His lips took in the sensitive bud of her nipple. A long, drawn-out moan came from her lips as her head lolled backwards.

He pulled on the other strap of her leotard and helped her arms out before he continued his attention to her breasts. Pushing away from him, Scarlett peeled off the leotard completely and let it drop to the floor around her ankles. Her tights and underwear followed, leaving a pool of nylon and cotton at her feet. Linc ran his hands up the flat plane of Scarlett's stomach until they rested on her breasts. Her body reacted to his touch in such a way that he thought he might burst right there, his need so strong.

He captured her mouth again, their tongues dancing and exploring as their lips pressed tightly together. She slipped her hand down and cupped the bulge in his pants, and he let out an unrestrained groan as she massaged him.

"Bedroom," he demanded in a husky voice, and he pulled away just long enough to follow her down the hall and into her tiny room. He laid her naked body on the bed and admired her exquisite physique. Her hand moved to cover her flat stomach. "Please don't hide from me. I want to see you. All of you."

She did as he asked but looked away. Linc knew she was shy but had a feeling there was more to it than that.

With deft hands, he quickly removed his own clothes.

She reached out a hand, urging him to her, and he gladly accepted. He lay next to her on his side, and she rolled so their warm bodies were pressed together, facing each other. They kissed and stroked and pressed against each other. Heat and lust flooded him.

He urged her onto her back and lowered his hand across her breasts, abdomen, and lower. It danced over the smooth patch between her thighs, his fingers teasing apart the slick folds of flesh to find the tight bundle of nerves at her centre. Scarlett clenched tightly as his thumb found her and started its slow assault on her senses.

He left her side just long enough to retrieve a condom from his wallet and roll it on his engorged cock. Even he was surprised by how big it appeared. Then again, he had never been so turned on by a woman like he was with Scarlett.

He positioned himself between her thighs and kissed her closed eyelids. "Tell me you want it," he murmured.

"I do." She practically moaned the words. "I want it so bad."

He sighed loudly as he entered her tight, slick pussy, and she arched her back as he entered even farther. It was as if their souls, as well as their bodies, were joining while he moved inside her, bringing them both quickly to climax.

Hers came first, hard and fast, and she clamped her eyes shut. Her whole body shuddered with release and she gripped him so hard he thought for sure her fingers would leave a mark. She might break him in two. It felt as if she were bursting apart at the seams.

Light flared behind his shuttered eyes as his own orgasm shattered him.

Spent, he collapsed against her and pressed a kiss to her cheek. She opened her eyes and stared straight into his. Pushing her hair from her face, he smiled at her.

"That was ..." She sighed as if she couldn't find the words.

"Fucking amazing is what that was," he said before rolling onto his back beside her.

She curled up against Linc, her long legs tangling with his. His arm slid around her, pulling her against his chest.

She smelled good. Right. *Perfect*. He could feel her heart pounding against her rib cage. His was going crazy, too.

Their hearts were beating a staccato dance together.

CHAPTER 11

*A*s the weeks passed, Scarlett and Linc fell into a happy rhythm. Instead of partying, Linc found himself spending his precious spare time with Scarlett and discovered joy in the simplest of activities such as evening strolls between the sprawling dairy farms or visits to their favourite beach at Caloundra.

Trivia night at the pub had become a regular occurrence for the happy couple and Linc had taken great joy in introducing Scarlett to his friends. On their most recent outing, Hamish and Greer had invited them to a Sunday afternoon barbecue at their place so they could all get to know Scarlett better.

"How old is the baby?" Scarlett asked as she clutched a bowl of salad in her hands and followed Linc from his car to the building that housed the coffee roastery Hamish had become famous for.

"He's about six months old I think." Linc got the

words out just before Hamish's huge brown dog let out a loud howl and wandered over for a sniff.

"Hello, Hercules." Linc scratched the dog behind the ear, right where he knew he liked it. Herc sat on his haunches and leaned into Linc's hand, his tongue rolling out in bliss.

A screen door opened, and Hamish appeared, followed closely by Greer, who was holding a bundle of happy baby on her hip.

Greetings were exchanged and Hamish took the salad from Scarlett. "I'll pop this in the fridge upstairs." He gestured to a staircase. "You guys go around back and I'll meet you there soon."

Greer led the way, Herc following close behind.

Greer bounced her son on her knee as she and Scarlett chatted as though they had been friends forever.

"What's his name?" Scarlett asked, and Linc noticed her hands clenched together in her lap. Her apprehension around the baby was obvious, and Linc wondered if this would always be the case, or if she simply needed more time to feel comfortable.

"This is Caleb." Greer kissed his head which had a great deal of fine brown hair covering it.

"He's growing up so quick," Linc said as Hamish handed him a beer.

"Sure is." Hamish grinned. "He'll be joining us on the golf course in no time!"

"Don't get too ahead of yourselves, boys." Greer

laughed. "The way he's taken to Freya's horse makes me think he might be more into equestrian than golf."

"Freya thinks he should ride in to the wedding. Really make an entrance," Hamish said.

"It certainly would. I hope someone leads the horse." Linc smiled.

Greer laughed. "As best man, I think that responsibility will fall to you."

Linc turned to Scarlett, who had a blank expression on her face. "These two are getting hitched in a month at Emerald Hills. That's the dairy farm where Greer grew up before heading overseas to cook at some of the best restaurants in Europe."

Scarlett's jaw dropped open. "Oh, wow. Congratulations. How exciting."

Greer reached over and placed a hand on Scarlett's knee. "You will come, won't you?"

It had been on Linc's mind to ask Scarlett, but he hadn't known if it was too soon or not to do so. Then she looked at him, and he knew he wanted her by his side. "Will you come? As my date?"

She smiled and nodded at him. "I'd love to." Then she turned to Greer and thanked her for including her.

"It's going to be such a great day." Hamish hugged his son and fiancée together. "I can't wait."

～

Scarlett watched the exchange between Hamish and Greer. The love between them was obvious and caused a great stirring in Scarlett's heart. She had been alone most of her life and was so used to her lifestyle that she wasn't sure she could live any other way.

But she would be lying if she thought seeing this happy family together didn't make her reconsider her opinion.

"Would you like to hold him?" Greer asked. She must have noticed the way Scarlett was watching them, letting herself imagine a life like theirs.

Scarlett was just about to make up an excuse when Greer held the baby out to her, giving her no option but to take the bundle of warmth.

Greer advised her how best to hold Caleb and soon Scarlett found herself in a not terribly uncomfortable position with Caleb's short legs straddling her hips while her hands cradled his neck.

The baby stared intently at her. Scarlett stared back at him, taking in his chubby cheeks and big brown eyes. He really was a beautiful thing. Not that Scarlett had much experience with little kids. With no siblings or friends with children, she was limited in her experience with and knowledge of them. All her students were school-aged—walking, talking little people. Not babies who relied on adults to provide for and look after them.

But this curious little chap seemed content to play

the staring game, even giving her a smile and a giggle, which tugged at her heartstrings.

Scarlett turned to see Linc deep in conversation with Hamish. Was he like his friends and ready to settle down and have a family of his own?

He caught her eye and smiled at her, his face giving nothing away. What would it be like to be a mother? To bring a baby of her own into the world?

Scarlett pushed the thoughts aside as Caleb started to fuss, and Greer took him off for a nap. Standing, she brushed down her shorts and joined the men, who were busy at the barbecue.

Sausages and steak sizzled on the grill. The smell drifted to her on the breeze.

"How do you like your steak?" Hamish asked, pointing to a large chunk of meat.

"Wow, I'm not going to be able to get through all that!" she said honestly while trying not to sound ungrateful.

Linc wrapped his arm around her waist. "Don't worry. I'll gladly finish off whatever you don't eat."

"I'll go get the plates," Hamish said. He handed Linc the tongs and made his way back into the loft.

Linc turned Scarlett in his arms so she could see his handsome face. "Sorry about putting you on the spot like that about the wedding." His voice was gentle and smooth. "You don't have to come if you don't want to."

"Are you taking back your invitation?" she teased.

"Not at all. I just don't want you to be uncomfortable."

She kissed his lips lightly. "Thank you for that. But I do want to come. It'll be fun."

He kissed her again. "Guess that makes us a real couple then," he murmured against her ear. "Never been one of those before."

"I'm pretty new at this too," she breathed out the words as she captured his mouth and kissed him. Heat and need built quickly through her.

Hamish politely cleared his throat and Scarlett broke the kiss. Her cheeks reddened with embarrassment. "Sorry."

"No need to be sorry," Greer said as she placed the salad on the table. "We're so thrilled for you two. You make such a great couple."

Scarlett looked at Linc and saw the adoration in his eyes.

She was so happy. She had never allowed herself to be happy like this before. She really did hope she wouldn't screw it up.

CHAPTER 12

*S*carlett studied herself in the full-length mirror. The colour was nice but was that fat bulging out of the back bodice?

She twisted to get a better view of the sleeveless midnight-blue gown. This was almost as bad as swim-suit shopping. All she could see were the imperfections —the lumps, bumps, and bulges, and her widening waistline.

Audrey knocked on the changing room door. "How's that one?"

Scarlett sighed. "Nope. I think I need something more conservative. With long sleeves."

"In the middle of summer? You'll boil."

Scarlett shrugged her way out of the close-fitting dress. She'd rather boil than give anyone a reason to laugh at or judge her. Hanging the dress up, she glanced over at the six other outfits she had already tried on and disliked. The pink was too short, the grey washed her out, and the lilac showed everything.

"How about that black one I showed you?" Scarlett called through the door.

"It was more of a mother-of-the-bride dress," Audrey replied from the other side. "Besides, you can't wear black to the wedding."

"Then maybe I shouldn't go at all." Perhaps this was just a sign that it was too early in their relationship to be seen out so publicly. People would look at her and wonder what on earth Linc saw in her. Better she stay at home or better yet, go to the gym and put in an extra workout. God knew she could use it. All the pasta and bread she had been eating with Linc was going straight to her hips.

"Don't be ridiculous. You can't chicken out now." Audrey tossed another dress over the changing room door. "Try this one. If you don't like it, we'll take a break."

They had already been shopping for hours. This was the fifth formal-wear store today. Maroochydore was running out of options.

Scarlett readjusted her strapless bra so it flattened out the bulge which had formed under her armpit, then she gathered the dress. It was a dark turquoise in colour with a high neckline, loose sleeves, and tie at the waist. She slipped it on and smiled. The flowing skirt came just below the knee, and the belted waistline showed off the curve of her waist . She turned to see herself from every angle in the mirror. All her bulges were covered, and it wasn't tight or clinging anywhere. This she could do.

"Well?" Audrey urged.

Scarlett opened the door and stood back so her friend could judge for herself.

"Wow." Audrey's eyes bulged. "That looks really good."

"Formal enough for a wedding?"

"For this wedding, yes. You could put some really cute heels with it and maybe even a hat—"

"No, no hat. We're not in England."

"Okay, but cute shoes at least."

Scarlett looked down at her bare feet which were misshapen and permanently blistered from her dancing career. "Closed in shoes. No one needs to see these toes."

Audrey threw up her hands in surrender. "Okay, if that's what you need. You really are too hard on yourself though. You are beautiful. Most women would love to have your figure."

Scarlett shrugged. "Other dancers in my company had better physiques . And better feet. I used to be able to wear things in the kids' section. Not anymore."

"Why don't we get this paid for, find some shoes, then go to Chloe's evening yoga class?" Audrey suggested. Her friend knew her so well. That was just what Scarlett needed after the exhausting day.

"Deal. You go start looking for some shoes while I get out of this." Scarlett closed the door and gave herself a final look. She was tempted to take a selfie, but experience had proved that dressing room selfies could be very harsh and critical, so instead she untied the dress and changed.

Everything would be fine, she kept telling herself. She would get her hair and makeup done so no one would see the dark bags under her eyes or the extra skin under her chin, which had appeared practically overnight.

She took a deep breath and let it out slowly. Everything would work out just fine. At least that was what she hoped.

As they left the shop, with the dress carefully wrapped in tissue paper, Audrey pulled Scarlett into a coffee shop. "I'm dying for some caffeine," she exclaimed.

After ordering their skinny cappuccinos they both sank, exhausted, into their chairs.

"Thank you for coming with me today. It means a lot to me." Scarlett smiled at her friend.

"Of course! My pleasure." Audrey's eyes lit up. "Remember those costumes we had to wear for *The Nutcracker*?"

"Oh, they were so scratchy!" Scarlett laughed at the memory. "Did you like being in the corps?" she said, referring to the group of dancers who were not principals or soloists.

Audrey nodded. "We didn't have quite the same pressure on us as you did—the lowest rung of the company, the nameless, faceless group who dance behind the major stars, out of the spotlight." She smiled. "I freaked out the day the email arrived. I'd been accepted into the Queensland Ballet Company. All of my hard work, the years of training and sacrifice, had paid off."

Scarlett remembered her days in the corps. How the shimmer of membership had quickly faded. Soon, just being one of the company wasn't enough. It was about moving up, getting noticed, winning solos and larger roles. The training got harder, the competition more fierce. "That last year I felt like I was running on a treadmill that only went faster: pushing myself harder just to stay in the same place. I danced every night until my toes bled and went straight back in the morning for more."

"Is that why you retired?"

"The truth is, I wasn't so certain I wanted this anymore—the work, the long hours, all the counting calories and missing out on normal life." She sighed. "Now I just want to go back to the stage. I miss it so much."

"Out of the full company of dancers, we all know only a small handful will ever graduate to be principals, dancing the big roles, and of them, maybe one or two in a generation will become prima ballerinas, the best of the best, praised and adored by all. You worked hard enough to be one of those dancers."

"I don't think I'd call myself a prima. Besides, most dancers peak in their late teens or early twenties, and by the time we're over twenty-five, our bodies can't keep it up any longer." She stared into her milky coffee. "They'd have kept me around another year in the back of the corps, just another face in the crowd. But we all know a ballerina has a limited shelf life."

And if you're not moving up the company ladder, sooner or later, you'll be moving out. From there, it was a slow slide to minor companies, touring smaller cities until finally, you admitted defeat and wound up teaching or quit ballet entirely—just another dancer who couldn't make the cut.

"Which is why teaching the next generation of dancers is so fulfilling." Audrey smiled, clearly proud of all she had achieved with her dance studio.

"It is amazing watching them improve so much and so fast."

"And you're helping to empower those boys and girls who want to make a career out of dancing. They see you and see it's possible for them too. Like Aimee."

"She is just the sweetest!"

"She looks up to you so much. I'm sure she wants to be you when she grows up."

Scarlett sipped her cappuccino, wondering why anyone would want to be like her. Her career had been her life. Everything she did or didn't do had been dictated by dance. Scarlett wouldn't wish that on anyone, especially happy, adorable Aimee.

Then again, Scarlett thought, if she could do it all again, would she really change anything?

CHAPTER 13

The Saturday of the wedding was a clear, warm day with a gentle breeze floating over the Maleny hills.

After her early yoga class, Scarlett prepared for the wedding by painting her nails, styling her hair into a chic updo, and putting on makeup.

She studied her appearance in the full-length mirror while she waited for Linc to pick to her up. Knowing people would be looking at her, interested to see who Linc had found appealing enough to give up his single life for, Scarlett had been extreme dieting all week. Her already low-calorie plan had been halved, giving her just enough energy to get through her classes and gym sessions while staying in ketosis so she would burn some fat. She had noticed a difference on her scale, but she found it hard to see any substantial difference in the mirror.

Knocking on the door made Scarlett pull her attention from scrutinising her backside, and she let Linc in. Dressed in grey pants with a matching waistcoat over a crisp white shirt, he looked like he'd stepped right out of a fashion magazine. The tips of her fingers tingled with the need to touch, to explore. Her blood pulsed harder when he was around, and her heart fluttered at the mere sight of him.

"You look great," she said, unable to move her eyes from him.

"So do you." He gestured to her body. "Just gorgeous."

Heat flushed her cheeks at the compliment, which she wouldn't let herself believe. She wondered again why he was with her when he could have any number of other prettier, sexier women.

He pressed a kiss to her forehead. "Nervous?"

She nodded ."It sounds like all of the hinterland will be there."

"Hamish and Greer do know a lot of people. Or at least their parents do."

After she locked the door, they walked out to Linc's car. As usual, Linc opened the passenger door and closed it once she was settled inside.

The scenic drive out to Emerald Hills past quickly. Scarlett's nerves got worse and worse with every metre. Was it too late to change her mind?

Cars were packed in the ample car park, and Linc found a spot under the shade of a gum tree. As they walked through the lot, she took note of what people were wearing. Sundresses and day suits in a variety of colours and fabrics, and many women were indeed wearing hats—although considering it was an outdoor wedding, she wondered if this was less of a fashion statement and more to protect against the harsh sun. While being grateful she had slathered on layers of sunscreen under her makeup, Scarlett hoped her pale skin didn't go too red today.

Linc held her hand and led her down a path beside the main restaurant to the area where the wedding would take place on a flat lawn with sprawling views of the Glasshouse Mountains. A large white marquee that reminded Scarlett of a circus tent had been erected, and people were milling about inside. As they got closer, Scarlett saw that hay bales with blankets on top had been set out for guests to watch the ceremony from. At the end of the alter was an arbour for the bride and groom to stand under and exchange their vows. Fairy lights and sprigs of native flowers adorned it.

"This is so beautiful," Scarlett said as she took it all in.

A waiter offered him a tray of sparkling wine and Linc accepted two flutes, then passed one to Scarlett. They clinked the glasses together before she took a sip. The bubbles fizzed all the way down Scarlett's throat.

Hamish waved at them from the arbour, and Linc led Scarlett up the aisle. As she walked the long path, she gazed about her. Would she make a similar walk one day? Would she ever wear the white dress and take those vows?

She shook her head. What silly thoughts to be having.

She sipped more of her bubbles and told herself to stop being so silly.

"Thanks for coming." Hamish gave Scarlett a brief hug.

"Congratulations," she said. "This looks amazing."

"Thanks. I wish I could take the credit but it's all Greer and Freya." Hamish went on to explain how Emerald Hills was becoming a very popular wedding venue for its amazing views and top-notch service. The menus Greer had designed were also a huge drawcard.

Linc showed Scarlett where to sit in the second row and returned to take up his best man duties next to the groom. Scarlett watched as a solo guitarist started playing an acoustic version of a popular love song and the wedding procession began.

Baby Caleb was carried up the aisle in the arms of an older woman Scarlett presumed was Greer's mother. He smiled as everyone gazed upon him. Next came Freya, looking stunning in a sky-blue dress. Her gaze caught her husband Justin's, and Scarlett smiled at the obvious love and affection they felt for one another.

Greer and her father walked slowly up the aisle. Her ivory gown was simple but stunning. Its strapless satin bodice hugged Greer's slim waist before giving way to a tulle-covered skirt that flared into a train and ended in pretty lace edging. A long, sheer veil was draped over her face and a bouquet of blue and white flowers were in her hand. As they reached the arbour, Scarlett couldn't help but stare at Linc, all confident and calm beside his best friend. Occasionally, he would look at her and give her a reassuring wink.

Vows were spoken, rings slipped on fingers, and a kiss exchanged that was so loving and heartfelt sniffles sounded from somewhere behind her. As guests rushed forward to offer their congratulations and take photos, Scarlett waited for Linc to return to her. Waiters came around with fresh glasses of sparkling wine and Scarlett helped herself to another.

As she took a sip she felt a brush against her hand, then Linc's little finger was hooked around hers. She stared at him, all chiselled chin and bedroom eyes, until a cheeky grin snapped her out of her stupor and returned her to the present.

Scarlett stepped forward and offered her congratulations to the couple as they passed.

"We're so glad you're here," Greer said after kissing Scarlett's cheek. "You look amazing by the way!"

Scarlett watched as the bride and groom continued to greet their guests. She gazed down at her dress. She looked okay. Not amazing. She was at least five kilos overweight and had had to go a whole size larger than usual to fit this dress.

Linc kept his arm draped around Scarlett's back as he introduced her to his friends, and they had a lovely time chatting as the sparkling wine continued to flow and appetisers were brought around.

By the time the dancing started Scarlett was feeling a bit tipsy. *That's what I get for starving myself for the last few days and then drinking.*

Scarlett and Linc watched people move onto the dance floor for a while then Linc held out his hand and she took it, and they joined the happy couples on the dance floor. He held her in a proper waltz pose, one hand holding hers and the other resting on the small of her back. They moved around the floor to the music. The other guests seemed to disappear as Scarlett became lost in Linc's eyes. He pressed his mouth close to her ear, his whisper shooting electricity down her spine. "You're beautiful."

His words jolted her back to reality and she sighed. "Please stop saying that."

He stopped moving and looked at her. "You are though."

Scarlett shook her head, loosening tendrils of hair that she had to brush away from her face. "No I'm not. I'm fat and ugly."

Linc frowned at her. "Why would you say that? It's not true."

Scarlett dropped her arms and took a step back. Barely able to keep her voice even, she almost cried the words. "Yes, it is, and you're a liar."

Before he could respond, she twirled on her heel and fled the tent, avoiding eye contact with anyone.

Linc was left on the dance floor, alone and stunned. He had suspected she had low self-esteem and his heart had clenched every time he'd seen her fight herself about eating food. Her demons ran even deeper, though, if she thought of herself as ugly.

He followed her out of the tent where stars and a full moon helped light his way. He found her a short distance away, resting against a wooden fence. Black and white dairy cows slept peacefully on the other side.

"Go away," she snapped when he stepped into her line of sight.

"Scarlett, come on. Talk to me." He moved slowly toward her.

She sniffed. "I want to go home."

Linc placed his hand on her shoulder, but she shied away from him. "Don't touch me."

Hurt, he withdrew his hand, fished his keys out of his pocket, and followed her to his car.

During the short ride home he attempted to reason with her again but was met with an icy silence.

When he pulled up at her door, he followed her out of the car. He needed to try one more time.

"Scarlett," he said. She stopped at the door and faced

him. "You are absolutely perfect the way you are. You are certainly not fat or ugly."

The moonlight highlighted the pain on her face. What had happened to her? What had made her think this way? Was this the penance for being a professional dancer? As much as he liked her, he wasn't sure he was strong enough to fight those demons inside her. Especially if she couldn't see them.

"I think you are absolutely the most attractive woman I have ever met, and it kills me that you can't see that for yourself."

Scarlett looked at him like he was delusional. "Stop lying to me. I know I'm not beautiful. I'm not that ballerina anymore. That was a mask I wore. Makeup and sequins."

Lincoln couldn't believe what she was saying. He ached to hold her in his arms until she saw herself the way everyone else saw her. The way he saw her.

"Just say it. I'm not good enough for you. I'm not now, and I never will be." Hurt and anger spiked her venomous words.

"That's not true. You are the only person I have ever wanted like this." He sighed and raked a hand through his hair. He was sick of this. Sick of her denigrating herself and not believing in her good qualities.

He couldn't fix her. No matter what he said or did, she would need to do the work herself. To value and appreciate herself.

"You know what, Scarlett?" He threw his hands up

in surrender. "No one can love you until you learn to love yourself."

He strode back to the car and turned on the ignition, hoping, praying she would follow him.

But when he looked back at the door, it was shut and she was nowhere to be seen.

CHAPTER 14

The next morning Scarlett woke up disoriented, like a dark fog had invaded her brain. She didn't want to get out of bed or to face the day—all she wanted was to go back to sleep.

So she did.

The day after that, her alarm woke her up. She had classes to teach, but not until ten. Normally she would jog to the gym and work out first, but today she wanted to go back to sleep. It was only intense hunger that finally got her to her feet.

After eating a small pot of Greek yoghurt, she felt slightly more herself. As she debated whether to go back to bed and wither away or to have a shower, her phone rang. She glanced at the screen to see it was Chloe.

"Hello," she answered, her voice raspy from not having been used for over a day.

"Scarlett, you missed yoga class last night. Are you okay?" The genuine concern in Chloe's voice sent Scarlett over the edge, and she burst into tears. Maybe people did care about her after all?

Chloe didn't even hesitate. "I'm coming over right now. What's your address?"

Scarlett made it to the door a few minutes later. Her eyes were puffy from sobbing and as soon as Chloe saw her, she hugged her tightly and whispered reassuringly in her ear.

They sat together on the couch and Chloe comforted Scarlett as she finally found the words to tell her what had happened and how she felt so unworthy of anyone's love.

"I want to help you," Chloe said. "If you'll let me?"

Scarlett knew the depression she was sliding into and didn't want to go there. Not again. Not ever.

She nodded, knowing she needed Chloe to help her find herself and to find healthy strategies to overcome her past so she could move on in the future. "Please help me."

Scarlett rolled her head as she came out of meditation. She was getting good at quieting her thoughts and focusing on her breath. Morning yoga with Chloe was part of her daily routine and after six weeks, she was reasonably happy with her strength, balance, and ability to focus on the positive.

She was still in the process of building her self-confidence. Chloe had connected her to an Internal Family Systems therapist, and after just a few short weeks they had uncovered some childhood trauma.

In one such session, Scarlett had remembered over-hearing her mother and teacher discussing how natu-rally talented a dancer she was. Her mother had then said words to the effect of *Scarlett isn't good at anything else so she if she wants to make anything of her life, this will have to be it.*

Scarlett hadn't realised how much those sorts of comments had affected her. How the food demands and constant pressuring had formed her into a woman who, without dance, felt worthless.

But remaining in the ballet company had not been an option. Her body had protested the long, gruelling hours, which in turn had spiked her anxiety that if she couldn't dance she couldn't be successful or happy doing anything else.

In meditation, she had opened her mind to other possibilities. Ballet was still her number-one passion and she found joy in teaching her young students moves and routines. These girls were flourishing and finding true joy in not only their dance classes but other activities such as soccer, netball, and academics.

With the knowledge of her wounds and a deep desire to improve her mental health and her life, Scarlett continued to work hard to become a better version of herself.

She stayed in her position, cross-legged on the floor, while the other participants packed up and left. She mentally ran through her day's schedule of teaching classes and errands to run. All that would wait until after she'd had breakfast with Chloe.

As the last student left, Scarlett rolled up her mat and gathered her things.

"You did really well this morning," Chloe said as she met her at the door.

"Thanks," she replied. "I feel really good today."

"You look good too." Chloe touched her arm where the muscles had become very defined and strong.

"Thanks." Scarlett was grateful for the compliment and no longer felt the need to shy away from positive feedback. Through therapy and mindfulness exercises she had been able to bust through some of her trauma and not let anxiety and self-doubt take over.

"I don't know about you but I could smash an eggs benedict."

Scarlett's stomach agreed loudly, and they both laughed as they headed up Maple Street towards Meredith's Café.

They waved hello to Meredith as they sat down at their usual table.

"How's therapy going?" Chloe asked quietly.

"Really good, thanks. Definitely found some wounds from my childhood." Her issues with being criticised and not being good enough had started at a very young age. Although she knew her family and teachers were doing the best they could with the knowledge they had, some of their words and actions had left a deep mark on Scarlett. Now that she recognised them, however, she was healing and building up the self-confidence she had been lacking.

A line to order started to form as the morning rush began. "My turn to queue." Scarlett rose from the table and joined the line, stepping forward as a man was also joining.

"Sorry." Scarlett stepped back and looked up to see who she was cutting in front of.

Linc looked just as surprised to see her as she felt. After a moment, he blinked rapidly and waved for Scarlett to take the spot in front of him. She hadn't seen him since the wedding, and seeing him now brought up all the feelings she had been avoiding.

"Thanks." She took a step forward and, not wanting to be rude, faced him. "How are you?"

Linc bobbed his head. "Good. Fine, thanks, and you?"

"Pretty good, yeah," she replied.

She pretended to read the menu on the wall when all she really wanted was to fall into his arms and kiss him.

Her turn came and Scarlett quickly ordered, paid, and took her table number. Then she turned to Linc. "It was nice seeing you."

His smile was unconvincing. "You too."

Scarlett slinked back to her seat. Was that how things were going to be now? Awkward as hell? In a town as small as Maleny, they were bound to cross paths every now and then. She didn't want to feel this much ... what was this feeling? Regret? Heartbreak?

Chloe reached over and gave her shoulder a gentle rub. "Is that the first time you've seen him?"

She nodded.

"How do you feel?"

Scarlett answered before she could think through her reply. "I miss him."

Chloe turned in her chair and looked at Linc as he collected his takeaway coffee and walked back past them. He spared her a quick glance as he moved toward the door.

"I bet he misses you too," Chloe said. "You have come so far, so quickly, but there is still a long way to go."

Scarlett swallowed, her eyes starting to burn with unshed tears.

"I don't know Linc all that well, but from what I've heard, he seems a pretty good guy." Chloe caught Scarlett's gaze. "Each of you deserves to be happy, and you might find a lot of happiness being together."

"You really think so?"

"I know twin flames when I see them." Chloe smiled. "Go get him."

Scarlett was up out of her seat before she could talk

herself out of it. After sprinting out the café door, she paused to see which way he had gone. She spotted his ginger hair easily a few shops away and took off after him. She didn't know what she would say or do, only that she had to tell him how she felt.

"Linc!"

He turned around and had to catch her when she didn't stop fast enough and just barely avoided splashing his coffee.

She rested her arms on his and sensed his strength and warmth around her. "I'm sorry."

"It's okay. I caught you," he replied, his arm still firmly planted around her waist.

"I mean I'm sorry about what happened. What I said and how I acted."

"Oh." Linc gazed into her eyes like he wanted to escape into them. "I'm sorry too."

"I've missed you so much." Scarlett moved farther into his embrace and curled her fingers into the hair at the back of his neck. "Have you missed me, too?" she whispered, her gaze fixed on his mouth.

His reply was a slow, tender kiss that said just how he felt more than any words could.

Being with him was like coming home for Scarlett. With Linc she was safe, protected, and adored for who she truly was. She understood that now and never wanted to lose it again.

"I love you Scarlett," he said the words against her lips and took her hands in his. Everything she wanted to hear was in his voice, and everything she needed to see was in the intensity of his eyes. "You are the most beautiful woman I know and it kills me that you don't see how stunning you are. Inside and out." He kissed her knuckles.

"I've been working on it. I'm doing a lot of yoga and getting therapy." Her voice was full of hope.

He brushed his fingers over her cheek. "We're one now. You and me." He kept his eyes on hers. "You insult yourself then you might as well be insulting me, too So please go easy on yourself. On *us*. Okay?"

"Okay." She promised.

He crushed his lips to hers, parting them and delving deep for a long kiss that set her pulse racing.

CHAPTER 15

Scarlett peeked through the curtains when she heard Linc pull up that evening. Pre-performance nerves tickled her spine, and she glanced around, making sure the scene was perfect.

Several candles were alight around the living room. The furniture had been pushed to the sides, creating an empty space in the middle.

Holding her silk dressing gown closed at the middle, she opened the door and ushered him in.

"Hi. What's this?" A grin started to spread across his face as he took in the candles and the music.

Scarlett touched her hair, carefully wrapped up in a bun. "I want to show you something." She moved into his arms and kissed him gently.

The sweet kiss soon turned deeper. Linc's hand slipped inside her dressing gown and slid against the satin negligee. Already her nipples—and more—were aching for his touch. He could turn her on in a heartbeat.

Panting, she moved out of his touch and directed him to a seat. "I want to show you the real me."

He sat in the chair while she changed the music to a piano sonata. Then she removed the dressing gown to reveal the silver satin negligee and white pointe shoes.

She moved across the floor, slowly and seductively. Her body warmed, and the glow she always felt when she danced spread through her.

The desire to dance had scratched at her senses for so long, burrowing deep in her skin and prickling at her so she couldn't ignore it. She lost herself to the music and moved in any way her body wanted her to. She was free, freer than she had ever been before.

Then she shook her hair loose and threw off the negligee so all she wore were her pointe shoes. She was entirely herself, open and vulnerable like she had never allowed herself to be. His gaze was hot and hungry as he looked from one breast to the other. She'd never felt more desired or sexy in her life.

Scarlett moved with an effortless grace, swanlike in her fluid yet precise movement. And when she threw off her clothes, Linc drank her in, mesmerised.

Each move was filled with raw passion and sensuality. He couldn't have looked away even if his life had depended on it.

He'd missed her so damn much he'd barely been able to think about anything else. Work had been his salvation, giving him something else to concentrate on, and he'd grabbed it with both hands.

Now she was back and offering her whole self to him and asking for nothing in exchange except his love. It was a gift he would never disrespect.

The music changed and she moved slowly toward him. Her legs shuffled as she rose on pointe. She bent down and kissed his lips before climbing onto his lap so that she faced him with her legs straddling his waist. His hands found her knees, and she shivered as his thumbs made small, gentle circles on the sensitive skin of her inner legs, his gaze still fixed on her perfect breasts.

She continued moving on his lap, gyrating her pelvis against his growing bulge. Breathless, he moved his hands to cradle each side of her head and moved her mouth to his. She opened to him, accepting the delicious heat of his lips and the play of his tongue.

"Your body is perfect," he groaned out. "You are perfect."

She stopped moving and they looked at each other for a long time. Their eyes spoke unsaid promises that they would always be there for each other. To support and protect no matter what.

"By the way, I forgot to tell you something." She smiled at him, and her face was so full of adoration it made his heart hiccup. "I love you too."

SARAH WILLIAMS

LOVE STORIES THAT WILL ROPE YOU IN

The Brothers of Brigadier Station

(#1 in the Brigadier Station series)

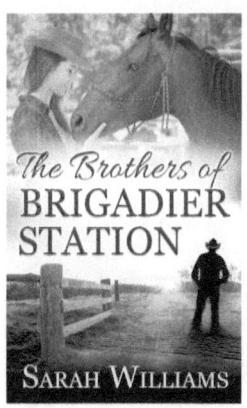

She came to the outback to marry the love of her life. She just didn't expect him to be her fiancé's younger brother.

When Meghan Flanagan, a vet-nurse from Townsville, moves to Brigadier Station in outback Queensland to marry the man of her dreams, she is shocked to discover that perhaps her fiancé isn't the man she wants waiting for her at the altar. The man she's destined to marry, just might be his younger brother.

Cautious of women after a disastrous past relationship, Darcy is happy living on his beloved cattle station, spending his spare time riding horses, going to rodeos and campdrafting. He didn't expect the perfect woman show up on his doorstep. Engaged to his brother.

With the wedding only hours away, Meghan must make the

decision of a lifetime. But, her betrayal could tear the family apart. She knows all too well the pain of losing loved ones and being alone.

Now that she has the family she so desperately wants; will she risk losing it all?

Buy The Brothers of Brigadier Station

The Sky over Brigadier Station

(#2 in the Brigadier Station series)

*He guards his heart. She yields to no man. Will a chance
encounter set a course for true love?*

Noah McGuire buries his demons deep inside. But when he's
forced to return home to Brigadier Station to collect his
inheritance, he can no longer avoid digging up his painful
past. With the wounds of childhood trauma reopened, his
world plunges into darkness until a beautiful pilot sets his
heart afire.

Riley Sinclair isn't afraid to fly against the wind. While the
spunky helicopter pilot's cattle herding business ruffles the
feathers of most men, the handsome Noah seems different.
But as demand for her skills grows, she worries that giving
into passion could keep her dreams grounded.

As their chemistry soars, an unexpected tragedy throws their lives and their budding romance into a tailspin.

Can Noah and Riley leave their baggage behind to let love fly free?

The Sky over Brigadier Station is the second standalone book in the captivating Brigadier Station Western romance series. If you like flawed characters, simmering scenes, and stunning Australian and New Zealand settings, then you'll love Sarah Williams' rugged tale.

Buy The Sky over Brigadier Station

The Legacies of Brigadier Station

(#3 in the Brigadier Station series)

Can Lachie be the father Hannah needs? And the man Abbie deserves?

Lachie McGuire is trying to make a fresh start. He's sobered up and is making amends for all the people he has hurt and the pain he has caused. But some of his past actions have consequences. Even if he doesn't remember them.

Needing her independence, single-mum Abbie Forsyth accepted a nursing position in the small outback town of Julia Creek and uprooted her daughter, Hannah from the only life she had ever known. Now, in the dusty, sun burned land they are creating a life together, just the two of them.

When Lachie is injured and needs medical assistance, Abbie is there for him. She's by his side every step of the way, including letting him stay with them while he recovers from surgery. But Abbie knows how volatile life with an addict can be and she has to think about her daughter's safety above her own growing affection for the handsome grazier.

Then tragedy strikes the small rural town and secrets begin to unravel…

Return to the Outback for the third instalment in the bestselling Brigadier Station series.

Buy The Legacies of Brigadier Station

The Dairy Farmer's Daughter

(#1 in the Heart of the Hinterland series)

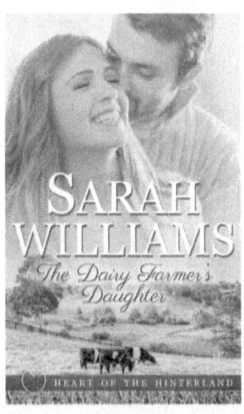

**He barely remembers his dad. She's all about community.
Can he let go of anger and harvest a passionate new life
with a sweet country girl?**

Brisbane, Australia. Justin Wheeler wishes it was just another
ordinary day. Living with his mum after her marriage fell
apart, the listless software developer grew up without a
phone call, a birthday card, or even a letter from his birth
father. So when the man dies and bequeaths him his rural
dairy farm on the Sunshine Coast, the bitter young man
reluctantly attends the funeral, intending to liquidate the
property.

Freya Montgomery brought her college know-how back
home. Intelligent and capable, the determined marketing pro
hopes to nurture her agricultural township while keeping the
handsome son of a deceased neighbor from selling out to a

developer. And when their instant attraction leads to a meeting with her family to discuss a possible lease, the optimistic beauty can't help but hope she can convince the smartly dressed stranger to stay.

Stunned when he falls head-over-heels for the vibrant farmgirl, Justin fears he may break her heart after he receives the perfect offer for the land. And though Freya is sure their chemistry is real, the sunny young woman worries the dark clouds of his simmering resentment at his late dad will leave her out in the cold.

Will the pair's passion survive and flourish on the milk of human kindness?

The Dairy Farmer's Daughter is the feel-good first book in the Heart of the Hinterland contemporary romance series. If you like fish-out-of-water heroes, opposites attract, and plenty of steam, you'll adore Sarah Williams's small-town tale.

Buy The Dairy Farmer's Daughter to inherit happiness today!

Bestselling author Sarah Williams spent her childhood chasing sheep, riding horses and picking Kiwi fruit on the family orchard in rural New Zealand. After a decade travelling, Sarah moved to Queensland to enjoy the endless summer, pristine beaches and tropical rain-forests.

When she's not absorbed in her fictional writing world, Sarah is running after her family of four kids, three dogs and an ever growing number of chickens.

She is Founder and CEO of Serenade Publishing, runs

writers workshops and retreats, mentors and supports her peers to achieve their publishing dreams.

To receive updates and free books, sign up for her mailing list.

www.sarahwilliamsauthor.com

facebook.com/sarahwilliamswriter
instagram.com/sarahwilliamsauthor
bookbub.com/profile/sarah-williams
goodreads.com/goodreadscomsarahwilliams

ACKNOWLEDGMENTS

My sincere thanks to the team at Serenade Publishing, my incredible editor Lauren Clarke and my cover designer Patti Roberts.

To Miss Dawn and the team at The Dance Academy for your patience and help. You are truly an inspiration.

A big thank you and much love to my family for all your support and for putting up with me while I work. Thank you Joshua, Toby, Raphaella and Arabella. I love you all.

And to you, dear reader. Thank you for choosing this book to read. I know there are many other distractions and entertainment options available these days, so thank you for joining Scarlett, Lina and me on this journey.

MORE FROM SERENADE PUBLISHING

A Dying Second Sun

by Peter A. Dowse

Winner Winner Chicken Dinner

by Sarah Jackson

A New Page

by Aimee MacRae

Middle Women

By Jack Garrety

Mim and Wiggy's Grand Adventure

By Jay McKenzie

For more information visit:

www.serenadepublishing.com